THE TWIN POWERS

ROBERT LIPSYTE

CLARION BOOKS
Houghton Mifflin Harcourt | Boston New York

Clarion Books
215 Park Avenue South
New York, New York 10003

Clarion Books is an imprint of Houghton Mifflin Harcourt Publishing Company.

www.hmhco.com

The text was set in Bembo Std.

Library of Congress Cataloging-in-Publication Data
Lipsyte, Robert.
The twin powers / by Robert Lipsyte.
pages cm. — (The Twinning project ; book 2)
Summary: Identical twins and mirror opposites Tom and Eddie share a "road trip" between planets and risk everything to save their father from the alien scientists.
ISBN 978-0-547-97335-7 (hardcover)
[1. Space and time—Fiction. 2. Twins—Fiction. 3. Brothers—Fiction. 4. Extraterrestrial beings—Fiction. 5. Ability—Fiction. 6. Science fiction.] I. Title.
PZ7.L67Tv 2014
[Fic]—dc23
2013043951

Manufactured in the United States of America.
DOC 10 9 8 7 6 5 4 3 2 1
4500490208

FOR DINAH STEVENSON,
A STAR ON ANY PLANET

Your sons are fine boys, John, but they are only thirteen years old.

They're our only chance, Dr. Traum.

That's an emotional response, John. Primary People like us are supposed to be rational. The boys are half human. They don't understand why their Earths must be destroyed.

Neither do I.

That's why you're my prisoner.

Give them a chance to find their powers and save their planets.

Why?

You owe it to them, Dr. Traum. For what you've put them through and for what they are going to have to do now.

ONE

THE aliens came back in the spring, just when I was beginning to think I'd never see Dad or my identical twin brother, Eddie, again. For years I had thought Eddie was imaginary, a voice in my head. When he came to Earth, a real live brother, it was one of the best days of my life. I thought we'd find Dad together and crack the mystery of just who we were.

It had been six months since we'd watched Dad disappear into the belly of the aliens' spaceship. I hadn't talked to Eddie in weeks. What was there to talk about? We were stuck on different planets—him on EarthTwo in 1958 and me on EarthOne in 2012—and nothing much had been happening on either one.

The day it all started again, I was ghosting through my morning classes, feeling down. Even Mrs. Rupp, the dumb history teacher with her boring timeline, couldn't get my juices going. She was on a topic that should have been interesting—nuclear energy—but Mrs. Rupp made us waste our time memorizing dates instead of learning stories that could explain why things happened. Usually I interrupt her because I'm bad, a troublemaker who likes to shake things up. I can't stand bullies or know-it-alls, even if they're teachers. But that day I kept my mouth shut. That's how down I felt. My best friends, Alessa and Britzky, thought I was sick.

At lunch, I hesitated before sitting at our regular table in the far corner of the cafeteria by the garbage cans, what I called the rebel table, because we dared to be different. I didn't want to be around Alessa and Britzky. They reminded me of everything I had hoped would happen but hadn't yet—my dream that the three of us, along with Eddie and his sidekick, Ronnie, plus Dad and Grandpa would set off again on our mission to save the Earths. If the Earths didn't destroy themselves by nuclear explosions or extreme weather, then the aliens would wipe us out because they were sure that the Earths would destabilize the entire universe and destroy them!

What made it even more complicated was that Dad and Grandpa were aliens themselves and Eddie and I were half alien, maybe the world's only halfies.

Could be time to get thrown out of school again, I thought. I could start my fourth middle school! I wondered if that would be a Guinness World Record.

When I did sit down, Britzky poked me and said, "Check out this dude."

The chatter and clatter of the cafeteria had faded away. Teachers had stopped talking on their phones. The kids at the jock, fashion, drama, digital, social, thug, and toasted tables were silent.

The only sound was the clop of boots as a short, skinny kid in a long black raincoat that flapped against his black jeans marched slowly toward us.

There was no expression on his pale face. He reminded me of someone. *Who?* I thought he was looking directly at me but I couldn't be sure because of the old-fashioned aviator shades he was wearing.

I whispered to Alessa and Britzky, "I thought you're not allowed to wear dark glasses in school."

"He's new," said Alessa, who worked in the school secretary's office. "His records are sealed."

"That means he just got out of juvie," said Britzky, his usually loud voice soft. "Or he's a government informer."

I thought of a third possibility. I wondered if they were thinking it, too.

Alessa said, "His name is Hercules."

"What kind of name is that?" I said.

Britzky whispered, "That could mean something. In the book *A Connecticut Yankee in King Arthur's Court,* the guy who hits the hero over the head is nicknamed

Hercules. And you know how the aliens love books by Mark Twain."

So Britzky *was* thinking about what I was thinking about. *Aliens!*

Hercules kept coming toward us. I wondered what he was covering up under his raincoat. Seventh-graders didn't carry automatic weapons into school. Not yet, anyway.

As usual, I was ready to rumble. That's the way I am. I felt for my Extreme-Temperature Narrow-Beam Climate Simulators. I had never used them in combat. They were two Sharpie-size nano composite rods. Scientists had invented them as part of the battle against global warming, but the army was interested in using them as weapons. So was I. I'd hacked the data and built them myself. They were my new favorite personal weapons. The data claimed either rod could stop a water buffalo. Together they could stop a herd. This might be a chance to see what the rods could do.

Hercules halted a few feet from the table. His voice was familiar. "Which one of you freaks is Tom Canty?"

Britzky jumped up and got between us. "What do you want with Tom?" He was in his old bodyguard mode. "You'll have to deal with me first."

"Ah, the paranoid loudmouth Britzky," said Hercules. How did he know about Britzky? "As Mark Twain said,

'It's better to keep your mouth shut and be thought a fool than to open it and remove all doubt.'"

The pimples on Britzky's forehead went neon, the way they always do when he's mad. He lowered his head but kept his eyes on Hercules and charged.

Hercules lifted his shades and stared at him with bright green eyes. We had seen such eyes before. They were alien eyes. Britzky froze, then turned around and walked back to his seat.

Hercules lowered his shades and turned to me. "So you must be the famous Tom Canty."

I stood up. "I'm Tom Canty."

Hercules smiled. "The YouTube star himself?"

The YouTube clip had gotten me kicked out of my second middle school. I had put a bully on his butt in the cafeteria with a blast from my TPT GreaseShot, my favorite weapon the year before. Someone had recorded the action with an iPhone and it was all over the Internet in seconds.

"Are you the Tom Canty who people mistakenly think founded Tech Off! Day?"

Mistakenly? How could he know that? It was my twin, Eddie, who'd come up with Tech Off! Day, in which everybody was supposed to switch off all elec-tronic devices for one day and get to know other people face-to-face. This had been last fall, when Eddie was on my planet pretending to be me and I was on his planet pretending to be him. Being Eddie wasn't easy for me. He's a nice guy.

But only the seven of us—me, Eddie, Alessa, Britzky, Ronnie, Grandpa, and Dad—plus the aliens—knew about the switch. Why had the aliens sent down this creepy guy? His glittery green eyes probably meant he was an alien, too.

"What do you want, Hercules?" I showed him some attitude. All around the cafeteria, kids were pointing their phones and tablets at us.

"I hear you think you're bad," said Hercules. "I've come to find out how bad."

TWO

BAD *enough!*

    I didn't say it out loud, yet Hercules nodded as if I *had* said it out loud.

But I didn't.

And he heard me.

I thought I could feel his eyes burning into me through his shades. I thought I heard an unspoken message from him. *This is a test, Tommy.*

I wondered if this was real or if I was going crazy.

You may be crazy, Tommy, but this is real.

I slipped both climate-stimulator rods out of my pockets.

Ahhh, Tommy and his toys.

I crouched and fired a blistering burst from the heat rod at the middle of Hercules's chest.

Feels like a taste of summer, Tom. What else do you have?

I fired a bitter burst from the cold rod.

A little autumn chill.

I thumbed both switches to maximum discharge and let him have the double blast between the eyes. No creature of this planet could stand up to that.

Of *this* planet . . .

Remarkable, Tom. At those temperatures, extreme heat and extreme cold feel about the same. Is that all you've got?

I thought, **What do you want?**

I'm disappointed. He actually sounded disappointed. *You and Eddie were supposed to find your powers, remember? To use them to save the Earths from destroying themselves.*

How?

By using your imagination.

I thought, **Imagination? What does that mean? Make up what I want to happen?**

That's a beginning, Tom. Something like this.

Hercules stared at my feet until a gassy whirl of atoms circled my ankles like a lasso. But if they were atoms, how was I able to see them? Was that one of my powers? The lasso tightened and pulled. I fell down hard on my butt.

Hercules laughed. The atoms disappeared. He reached out his arms, and a stream of liquid molecules sprang from his hands and began thrashing its way toward me.

Think of something, Tom! I said to myself.

I imagined as hard as I could. I focused my mind on

creating a wall of neutralizing ions that would repel the stream of molecules.

The stream slapped against my wall, fell away, and disappeared.

Good job, thought Hercules.

I glanced around. The cafeteria was buzzing as students and teachers jostled one another to get good angles for their cameras. Pictures of Hercules and me would be all over the Internet in seconds, if they weren't already.

Stay in the now, Tom, thought Hercules.

That's what Grandpa says when he wants total attention. Was Hercules making fun of me or giving me advice?

I heard a low hum, like air conditioning or a distant airplane, and I could feel waves banging against me like a dry surf. Hercules was building a little tornado to knock me down.

If he can do it, so can I, I thought.

You think?

I turned off every other thought in my head until all my energy was focused on churning the air around me, beating it with propeller blades, shaping it into a funnel.

Then I sent the tornado right at Hercules.

It took so much effort that I stopped breathing and blacked out for an instant. When I came to, I was swaying on my feet and Hercules was flying backwards into the drama table. Those actors shrieked as their trays flew. They were pelted with airborne food. There was screaming and cheering throughout the cafeteria, teachers bellowing for the nurse, kids standing on tables.

Hercules stood up slowly. He was smiling. One of his bright green eyes winked.

He thought, *As Mark Twain said, "The secret of getting ahead is getting started."* He turned and marched out of the cafeteria.

I was trembling so hard that Alessa and Britzky had to hold my arms to keep me from collapsing. But I felt great.

I said what we all knew. "It's finally happening. They're back."

THREE

WAS still beat from the battle with Hercules when I dragged myself out to the backyard garden that evening. I waited a long time for the clouds to move and the double star to double-blink, our signal. I've talked to Eddie like this since back when I thought he was imaginary. Eddie transmitted first.

'Sup, bro?

You have to talk like that?

Like what?

After he'd visited my planet, Eddie had started trying to sound like a twenty-first-century rapper instead of the 1958 Boy Scout that he is. Sometimes it bugged me.

Never mind. They're back, Eddie. One of them showed up at school today.

What happened?

We had a fight.

You okay?

Yeah. It'll be on YouTube.

YouTube hasn't been invented here yet.

Right. Sorry.

What was the fight about, Tom?

It was a test of my powers.

What powers?

I'm starting to find out, Eddie. You're supposed to be working on yours.

I know. Ronnie and I talk about it all the time.

So what have you done?

Oh, man, there's so much going on, with Boy Scouts, basketball—we won conference—now baseball practice . . .

We have to do something, Eddie. Dad's still a prisoner and we haven't done squat.

I know. But like what?

We're half alien, right? We're supposed to have special powers.

But what are they, Tommy?

He said we have to use imagination.

Who said?

The alien. Eddie, are you listening?

How do you use imagination?

Imagine what you want to happen until it happens.

What does that mean, Tommy?

Everything has to be spelled out for Eddie.

The way I figure it, Eddie, we've got to imagine what we

want to happen, not what we think will happen or what we're afraid will happen.

That's a lot of stuff to think about.

I lost it then. Sometimes it's really hard to get through to my brother. *I gotta go.*

No, Tommy, wait . . .

Mom just came outside.

Okey-doke. See you later, alligator.

I had lied about my stepmom coming outside. As usual, she was away, traveling for her job. I just didn't want to talk to Eddie anymore. He's my twin and I love him, but sometimes he can be such a dumb jock that it makes my teeth hurt.

FOUR

A t baseball practice, the fellas were talking about the Brooklyn Dodgers and the New York Giants. Last season, most of us had rooted for either the Dodgers or the Giants, but then both teams had walked out on us, moving to California. We were ticked off. How could we live in New Jersey and root for the Los Angeles Dodgers or the San Francisco Giants?

I'm team captain, so I had to come up with a way to get my players' minds back on *our* games. I said, "Let's root for the New York Yankees because they stayed!"

There were grumbles and boos, but I could tell that they would at least think about it. I reminded them that the Yankees were a great team—they had Mickey Mantle, Yogi Berra, and Whitey Ford—which seemed like a pretty smart thing to say. I thought it was the kind of thing Tom would have come up with. I know that

Tom is smarter than me, and it's okay. I love my brother even though I can tell that sometimes he gets annoyed with me for not being smarter than I am. That hurts. It isn't as though I ever point out that Tom can barely catch a ball.

The coach was late, so I divided the team for batting and fielding practice. "Enough about the Dodgers and Giants, fellas. The only team that really matters is the Nearmont Raiders."

I got a cheer out of that. "Raiders rule!" The players trotted out to the field or lined up behind the plate.

When the coach finally showed up, he had a guy with him. Coach yelled, "Listen up, Raiders. I want you to meet Hercules."

Somebody laughed and shouted, "Can he hold up the world?" because we were studying mythology in English class. But we all shut up when we got a good look at him. He was weird—short and skinny, with greasy black hair that stood up. Even though it was a chilly spring day, Hercules wore a sleeveless undershirt, gym shorts, and rubber shower sandals. And aviator shades. Coach would never let any of us come to practice like that. What was special about this guy? What position did he play?

Hercules walked right up to me. I didn't think I'd ever seen him before but there was something familiar about his face. He peeked over the tops of his shades. His bright green eyes gave me a chill. Alien eyes.

"The great Eddie Tudor, Captain All-Sports," said Hercules in a sarcastic voice that also seemed familiar. He picked up a bat and ball and pointed to shortstop, my regular position when I wasn't pitching. "Let's see what you got."

I didn't like being ordered around like that. I looked at Coach. He grinned and nodded. He looked as if he was in some kind of a trance. An alien could do that. Tom had said they were back.

I punched my glove and trotted to short. This was my territory. I felt sure of myself here.

Hercules twirled the bat overhead, threw the ball so far up into the air that it disappeared for a moment, then slapped an easy grounder right at me. *Too easy,* I thought as I sidestepped into its path. Just as the ball was about to skip into my glove, it popped straight up in the air, then blooped over my head into center field.

"Bad bounce, Eddie," said Hercules in a fake-friendly voice. "Try this."

The next grounder was a sharp grass-cutter to my left, the kind of hit I usually gobbled up. I moved over quickly and stretched out my arm so my glove would block the ball. Two inches from my glove, the ball snaked left and into the outfield.

"Keep your eye on the ball," said Hercules.

That frosted me but I didn't let it show.

The third hit off Hercules's bat was a line drive right at me. I braced myself. When the ball smacked into my glove, I clapped my right hand over it. But once in my glove, the ball picked up speed and power. It drove me backwards. I lost my balance and fell on my can.

Hercules laughed. So did the coach and the team. I kept a poker face. *Never let them know they got to you.*

Then I heard the high voice of my little sidekick, Ronnie, from the bleachers. "You caught it, Eddie—that's all that counts."

I gave him a little nod. Ronnie was a good guy, always trying to encourage me. We mostly talked about the past now. Waiting for the aliens to return had made us buggy. At least I had my teams. Ronnie didn't seem to have a life. I was getting tired of Ronnie's shaggy blond hair flapping next to me, his face always so serious. *He'll really be excited when I tell him the aliens are back,* I thought.

I hopped up off the ground and fired the ball right at Hercules's head. *Let's see what* you *got.*

Hercules didn't budge. Just before the ball smashed into his puss, he reached out and plucked it from the air like an apple off a tree. He tossed it back to me. I grabbed at it as if it might fly off again, but it was just a regular easy toss. Hercules grinned. He had gotten to me.

"I hear you think you're a pitcher, Captain Eddie," he said. He strutted to home plate.

I marched out to the mound. *Give him some heat, then the curve.* I didn't bother to warm up, just reared back and fired the fastball.

Hercules slammed it so far, it would have been a home run in Yankee Stadium. The team cheered.

"Is that your best pitch?" said Hercules. "Don't you have any imagination?"

Imagination? I thought.

You heard me.

It was as if Hercules had picked the question right out of my mind. Then he sent another message back. *As Mark Twain said, "Reality can be beaten with enough imagination."*

I remembered that Tom had told me to use my imagination. I was beginning to understand what he'd meant.

I waved Hercules back into the batter's box. Then I reared back as if I were going to throw another fastball, but I switched my grip in mid-wind-up and tossed the curve. Just as the pitch reached Hercules, I imagined that it dropped suddenly and spun left. I concentrated as hard as I could, focusing all my energy on the drop and the spin.

Hercules swung and missed so hard that he wrapped himself into a pretzel.

The team cheered me this time. Ronnie let loose his shrill whistle.

Hercules straightened himself out and nodded. *Good start, Eddie. Now practice hard. Next time, it won't be practice.*

He marched off the field.

FIVE

RONNIE
NEARMONT, N.J.
1958

I HAD to grip the grandstand seat to keep myself from running out to Eddie on the mound. The waiting was over. No question. The aliens were back! I hoped Eddie understood that. He was the greatest guy in the world, but sometimes it took him a little while to figure things out.

When practice was over, I hung around the locker-room door waiting for Eddie. He was surrounded by his teammates, who were slapping his back and saying things like "Way to go, Cap'n Eddie." I trailed them by a few feet, feeling like a fifth wheel. Eddie didn't seem to want me around so much nowadays. Eddie and his grandpa had given me a place to stay so I wasn't homeless anymore, but I was wondering if it was time to hit the road again.

Finally, Eddie was alone.

"He's one of them, Ronnie," he whispered.

"I think so too."

"What do you think he wants?"

"To get you working on your powers, Eddie."

"Why would they want that? They're our enemies."

"Not all of them. Not your dad. Or Grandpa."

Eddie stopped. He screwed up his face and cocked his head the way he does when he's thinking hard. "You're right. You think Dad could have sent Hercules?"

"Maybe." I didn't really think so—Dad was Dr. Traum's prisoner—but I wanted to keep the conversation going since Eddie and I hadn't been talking much lately. "It was like he was pushing you to be better, Eddie. The way a coach does. Or a good teacher."

Eddie nodded. "First thing, I thought Coach brought him to light a fire under me for the season. But those green eyes. And he looked familiar."

"Like Dr. Traum," I said.

"That's it!" Eddie whacked my shoulder. It hurt but it felt good, as if we were a team again.

We looked at each other and shivered. Dr. Traum scared us. He had suddenly appeared in our school six months ago and taken over the jobs of both the football coach and the school psychologist. Very unusual. Later we found out that at the same time, he'd showed up at Tom's school on EarthOne and taken over the jobs of guidance counselor and music teacher. Aliens could be in two places at the same time. Grandpa said Dr. Traum was using those green eyes to transmit back to the alien planet, Homeplace.

In those days, Dr. Traum had been hunting Tom and Eddie's dad, John Canty. Mr. Canty was the leader of the alien underground, trying to help human beings save their planets—either from self-destruction or, we'd found out later, from the aliens led by Dr. Traum.

Dr. Traum had used Tom and Eddie as bait to find their dad. It had worked. Mr. Canty gave himself up so Tom and Eddie and the rest of us could go free.

After Tom and Eddie's dad was captured, Dr. Traum disappeared from both schools. So why would Dr. Traum send someone down to us now? What was he plotting?

Everything was a mess.

When the twins had switched identities the year before, Eddie slipping to EarthOne in the year 2011 and Tom slipping to my planet, EarthTwo, in the year 1957, I'd had no idea what was going on. All I knew was what I was told—the best friend I knew as Eddie Tudor had hit his head in a fall at Scout camp and couldn't remember anything. He needed me to be like his guide dog in school. I liked that—I liked doing something for Eddie for a change. I didn't always like the way that Eddie acted, though. I'd figured it was because of the accident, but it was because Eddie was really Tom pretending to be Eddie! It's confusing.

After Dr. Traum captured Tom and Eddie, it had been up to me to bust them out of the insane asylum where they were prisoners and drive them to safety. That was the best day of my life. I had never felt so strong and big and smart. I'd do anything to feel that way again.

When the real Eddie finally came back to EarthTwo, we lived together in Grandpa's house and talked all the time about joining up with Tom and his friends, defeating the aliens, and freeing Eddie's dad.

Now I wondered if it was ever going to happen.

"What do we do now, Ronnie?"

"Work on your powers."

"That's what Tom said."

"You talked to him?"

"Last night. He said he had a fight with a guy in school."

"Who?"

"A skinny little guy in sunglasses."

"Was it Hercules?"

"Could have been. The guy told Tom to work on his powers. Use his imagination."

"This is good news, Eddie. They're back. Something's going to happen."

"You really think so?"

"Does Elvis have a pelvis?" I knew that would make him smile. It did. He put a hand on my shoulder.

"Maybe we'll get to see Dad and Tom soon."

SIX

HADN'T seen Tom so excited in months. For the next forty-eight hours, we talked and texted about Hercules and the aliens and saving the Earths. For the first time in a long time, we went back and forth to school together. The three of us walked the halls like a six-legged creature. We kept saying the same things over and over.

"It's going down," Tom said. "Maybe we'll get to see Dad and Eddie soon."

"Hercules was just a test," said Britzky.

"For what?" I said. That was my line.

"To see if I'm ready," said Tom.

"You better be ready," said Mrs. Rupp, the history teacher. We hadn't heard her come into the room. She put her laptop on the desk and yelled, "It's time for . . . Mrs. Rupp's . . . Timeline!"

The class groaned. Mrs. Rupp makes us memorize

dates. She says you can't understand history unless you know the order in which things happened. She says that there are people who don't know that there are nearly a hundred years between the Revolutionary War and the Civil War. She tries to make it into a demento game show, but it still isn't fun.

Now we were studying the history of nuclear power, for bombs and for everyday energy, which could have been interesting, but not on Mrs. Rupp's Timeline. No stories, just dates.

"Oh-kay-doh-kay, here we go," she shouted as her timeline flashed from her laptop to the screen in the front of the room. "Let's look at nuclear testing, from July 16, 1945, the Trinity test in New Mexico, to January 14, 2012, when the Science and Security Board of the *Bulletin of the Atomic Scientists* set the Doomsday Clock to five minutes to midnight. Where did we leave off, anybody named Alessa?" She pointed at me.

Britzky saved me. "August 1953, when the Doomsday Clock was set to two minutes to midnight."

"Righterooni!" yelled Mrs. Rupp. "Next?"

"Why two minutes?" asked Tom.

"The scientists thought the world was really close to nuclear war and maybe total destruction," said Britzky. "That was based on—"

"That's enough, Todd," said Mrs. Rupp. "We have

many years to cover and this is only one blip on one of our timelines."

"But it's interesting," said Tom. "My dad always said history should be stories."

Mrs. Rupp glared at him. She'd never liked Tom. "Your father can tell you all the stories he wants, but we're here to learn the order in which things happened."

"But I want to know why they happened and how they happened and what happened afterward," said Tom.

"Me too," I said, to give Tom some support.

Mrs. Rupp's face got stony. "Moving right along. Next?"

Tom said, "May 12, 1958. A thermonuclear explosion in New Mexico."

Mrs. Rupp checked her laptop and shook her head. "It's not on my timeline. It couldn't have happened."

"Maybe there was a cover-up," said Britzky.

"It was a big secret," said Tom. "The government didn't want people to know about it."

Mrs. Rupp looked confused and angry. She was figuring out what to do when I jumped in. "C'mon, guys. We've got another sixty years before they set the Doomsday Clock back to five minutes before midnight."

Britzky and Tom gave me the dirty looks they always do when I try to smooth things over. But they're always glad afterward when nobody gets punished.

"That's good, Alessa," said Mrs. Rupp. "But let's not get too far ahead of ourselves."

"See you all in sixty years," said Tom, putting his head on his desk and snoring.

Mrs. Rupp ignored him and tapped her laptop, and the timeline moved on.

SEVEN

T HAT was pretty dumb," Alessa said to me on the
way home. "Mrs. Rupp hates to be dissed."

"I couldn't help it," I said. "It just popped into
my head, like a tweet. I don't know where it came from.
I've never heard of a thermonuclear explosion in 1958
before."

"There was a rumor on a conspiracy website," said
Britzky, "of a blast that got hushed up."

We walked for a while in silence. I wondered if someone had transmitted that information to me.

Hercules? Dr. Traum? Dad?

Why?

I could sense that Alessa and Britzky had something
on their minds. I could almost hear their brains buzz.
Finally I said, "What?"

Britzky looked at Alessa. They'd been talking behind
my back.

She said, "Maybe it's time we helped you work on your powers."

I was annoyed because she was right about that. It was time. Maybe past time. I'd let things slip the past six months, feeling hopeless.

But I didn't want her to feel too smart. "You know what I'm going to work on first?" I said. "Seeing through clothes."

Alessa gasped and Britzky said, "He's messing with you," and gave me an elbow.

Alessa changed the subject. "You know what's weird? All those kids recording Tom and Hercules in the cafeteria, and nothing's showed up on YouTube."

"The aliens wiped them out, probably with sunspots," said Britzky.

We just looked at him. It sounded crazy, but he's usually right about crazy stuff like that.

We were at my house and I waved them in. I wanted to keep us together for a while. "Grandpa's got peanut butter ice cream."

We were at the kitchen table spooning out the ice cream when Grandpa walked in. He didn't say hello. He looked serious. "Stay in the now," he snapped.

"That's what Hercules said," said Alessa. I had told her some of the thoughts Hercules had sent me during our fight.

"It's a Primary People expression," said Grandpa. "Hercules made contact with Eddie yesterday too."

"Is something going to happen?" said Britzky.

"It's already happening," said Grandpa. "Look out the window."

I was closest and got there first. A gray metal spider with spinning helicopter blades hovered over the house.

"A drone," said Britzky. "It's the kind the government uses in Afghanistan to spy on people and sometimes drop bombs."

"Why would the government send a drone to spy on us?" said Alessa.

"It's got something to do with Hercules," I said.

We all looked at Grandpa, who nodded. "The government must have found out that aliens are back in contact with Tom. The drone is going to shadow Tom, shadow all of us, in hopes that we'll lead them to the Primary People and Homeplace."

"We need to get to Homeplace," I said. "And free Dad."

It got quiet. I felt excited and scared. Britzky was staring at his big knuckles and Alessa was thumbing her cell. I could tell they were feeling excited and scared too. For six months we'd been waiting for something to happen, and now it looked as if something *was* happening.

"First thing," said Grandpa, "Tom has to learn how to use his powers. We have to help him. It doesn't happen overnight. Tom and Eddie are the only half Primary People, half human beings in existence, maybe the only ones ever. That rare combination of human imagination and Primary People rational intelligence is our only chance."

"To free Dad?" I said.

"To keep the Earths from destroying themselves," said Grandpa.

We got quiet again. I was wondering and I knew Alessa and Britzky were wondering too: How could one old man and a bunch of thirteen-year-olds save the worlds?

EIGHT

WE were talking about our favorite TV show, *Wagon Train,* while Grandpa made scrambled eggs for breakfast. Ronnie had really dug the last episode when the wagon master, played by Ward Bond, met his old girlfriend. I told them I'd thought it was sappy—and didn't have enough action.

"I liked it too," said Grandpa.

"Because it was about an old guy," I said.

We always kidded around like that.

After breakfast, Ronnie and I cleared the table and washed the dishes while Grandpa spread out the special map he keeps hidden away. He was planning a summer vacation for us, driving out to New Mexico. We would tell people we were going to visit Indian pueblos, but the real reason we were going was to check out the area where there had been rumors of an alien spaceship and nuclear testing. Ronnie and I wondered if it was a

Primary People thing, but Grandpa didn't want to talk specifics. We thought it was because he didn't trust us to keep our mouths shut.

I was excited about the trip but I didn't enjoy having to look at maps. Also, I was anxious to get to baseball practice. I was supposed to work on my pitching that day, and Ronnie was keeping a chart of my balls and strikes, as well as what kind of pitches I threw. I was working on a curve ball. I wanted to get better, especially after the duel with Hercules.

"Okay," said Grandpa, stabbing at the map with his finger. "Here's where we're going. Culebra de Cascabel. It's in a valley in the desert. The coordinate numbers are 106:06W and 34:19N. I want you to remember that."

"I can't remember that," I said.

"You can," said Grandpa. "Don't try to memorize it. Just look at it and let it print itself onto your brain."

"You can do it, Eddie," said Ronnie. He was always cheering me on. "Like you remember football plays."

"It's important," said Grandpa.

I looked at the map and recited, "Culebra de Cascabel. It's in a valley in the desert. The coordinate numbers are 106:06W and 34:19N."

"Excellent," said Grandpa.

"I forgot it already."

"It's embedded in your brain."

"How do you know?" I said.

"It's in the Primary People part of your mind."

There was a heavy knocking outside. Grandpa folded up the map and stuck it inside his shirt before he went to the door. He came back with two men in dark suits and hats. Grandpa gave us a warning look. "Eddie, Ronnie, these are federal agents."

My dog, Buddy, growled at them.

"Like the FBI?" I said.

"I hope you can help us out, Eddie," said one of them, ignoring my question. He flashed his badge and ID card at me too fast to read. "I'm Agent Smith. This is Agent Jones."

Ronnie asked, "You hunting Communists?"

"We're not allowed to discuss the case," said the agent, winking. "What can you boys tell us about this fellow Hercules?"

Both agents pulled out notebooks and pens.

Be careful, thought Grandpa. *Nothing about aliens.*

Grandpa doesn't think I'm so smart either. Just like Tom.

"He showed up at baseball practice," I said. "You should ask Coach."

"We talked to your coach," said Agent Jones. "He

said he didn't remember. He said he had a headache and the whole practice was kind of a blur. What do you remember?"

"You think there was something strange?" said Agent Smith.

"For a skinny little guy, he could hit a ton," I said.

They nodded and wrote that down. "Anything else?" said Agent Smith.

Grandpa said, "Boys'll be late for baseball practice."

"We're going to have to take Eddie to headquarters," said Agent Smith. "Give him a lie-detector test."

"Eddie never lies," said Ronnie.

"We'll find out," said Agent Jones.

"I'm not lying about anything," I said. I felt hot and angry.

"What do you think he's lying about?" said Ronnie. "Let's see your badges again."

Before I knew it, each agent had one of my arms and was pulling me toward the door. Buddy went to bite them, but Ronnie grabbed him.

"Where's headquarters?" said Grandpa.

"Downtown," said Agent Jones.

"When will you bring Eddie back?" said Ronnie.

"When he tells us what we want to know," said Agent Jones.

Stay calm, thought Grandpa. *Remember, you have powers.*

Outside, Agent Jones got into the back seat with me. Agent Smith drove. Neither of them said a word all the way into the city. My mouth was dry. I took deep breaths and held them for a count of ten. That's what Coach says to do if we feel nervous before an at bat.

We pulled up to a dumpy-looking hotel near the river.

"Is this headquarters?" I said.

They didn't answer. They pulled me through the hotel lobby and into an elevator. We got off at the fourth floor. The hall smelled of cigarette smoke. Agent Smith opened a door to a room containing a bed, some chairs, a television set, and a bathroom. It reminded me of a hotel room in a movie we'd watched on TV. In the movie, the cops were hiding a witness so he could testify before the grand jury. But the gangsters shot him through the window. I told myself to stay away from the window.

"Take off your shirt, pants, and shoes," said Agent Jones.

When I didn't move, they pulled off my shoes and socks and then my plaid shirt and chino pants.

"Just relax, Eddie," said Agent Smith. "Don't open the door for anyone. We'll bring you some lunch in a little while."

"Why am I here?" I said. I didn't like the whine in my voice.

"It's for your protection, Eddie," said Agent Smith.

"From who?"

They walked out with my clothes and locked the door behind them.

I sat on the bed, trying to think, but my mind was spinning like a fishing reel. It was hard to concentrate. This had something to do with Hercules, so it had something to do with aliens. Were these guys hunting aliens? I was getting scared again and the deep breaths weren't working, so I turned on the TV. I usually never watched TV in the daytime. Now I tuned in to a game show where you had to answer questions so you could connect the dots on a picture of a famous person. I couldn't answer any of the questions, which got me so mad that I wanted the TV set to blow up. Imagining the TV set blowing up calmed me down. In fact, it felt so good that I stared at the set until my eyeballs felt hot.

The TV set blew up.

The door burst open and the two agents ran in. "What's going on in here?"

I imagined blowing on the burning TV set to fan the flames like we do in Boy Scouts to get cooking fires going. It was fun. Then I imagined sparks from the TV fire landing on the bed and turning it into a bonfire.

A fire alarm sounded. One of the agents ran out of

the room and came back with a fire extinguisher. He blasted the TV set. The other agent began beating on the blazing bed with a blanket.

I took off, barefoot. I raced through the hall to the stairs, then four flights down to the lobby. I didn't have any plan except to get out of there.

In the lobby, people turned and stared. I realized I was wearing only a T-shirt and boxer shorts. Two guys in dark suits—looking a lot like agents Smith and Jones—shouted and ran after me.

A yellow taxicab came screaming down the street and pulled up in front of a line of cabs at the hotel entrance. A back door flew open. "Get in," the driver shouted. I jumped into the cab and it screeched into traffic before I had even closed the door.

"Nice going, Eddie," said the driver in a familiar voice. "As Mark Twain said, 'Action speaks louder than words but not nearly as often.'"

When he turned around, I saw it was Hercules. Whose side was he on, anyway?

NINE

HERCULES drove fast, making sudden turns that tossed me around the back seat. He was nodding as if he was listening to directions in his head. Was he getting a transmission from Homeplace? Was he telling Dr. Traum—or even Dad!—about what had just happened? That I was finding my powers and using them? That I understood imagination?

After a while, he pulled the taxi to the curb alongside a park. He turned around and lifted his shades. His green eyes were glittering.

"The word on you, Eddie," said Hercules, "is nice guy, lightning reflexes, but your elevator doesn't go all the way to the top."

"Who said that?" I was ticked off. "Tom?"

"You could learn a lot from Tom. Of course, he could learn a lot from you." Hercules got out of the cab and opened the back door for me. He was wearing a black raincoat and boots. He threw the car keys into the bushes. "We can always jack another one. Let's book."

I followed Hercules into the park. There were long-distance runners on the dirt trails and women pushing baby carriages on the grass. It looked friendly. I don't go into the city much, so I had no idea there were such big parks besides Central Park. I followed Hercules deeper into the park, off the paths and into groves of trees. I watched where I was stepping in the high grass. Snakes.

"No snakes around here," said Hercules, as if he was reading my mind. I hated that.

"I'm not afraid of snakes," I lied.

"Tom's scared of them, too."

"Where we going?"

"To Tom's planet. Get Tech Off! Day rolling. There's a place near here where you can slip to EarthOne." And then, as if I didn't know, he added, "That's Tom's planet."

"You think I'm a dodo?" When Hercules didn't answer, I said, "What about Ronnie and Buddy?"

"They're on their way." He stopped and gestured at a pack of tough-looking kids sitting in an open field, smoking and drinking beer. They had baseball bats. "First, you've got a problem to solve, Captain Eddie."

"Is this another test?"

"Life is a test, Eddie. Now, go straighten them out. A

Dudley Do-Right like you has to be against ballplayers smoking and drinking."

"Who's Dudley Do-Right?"

"Another heroic dimwit. A little after your time."

I decided to let that go. "That's not my team."

"They just picked you," said Hercules.

The guys had noticed us. Or at least me—Hercules had disappeared. They nudged each other, grinned, and slowly stood up. They were older than me and they looked mean.

"Me against all those guys?"

I could hear Hercules even if I couldn't see him. "As Mark Twain said, 'To believe yourself brave is to be brave; it is the one only essential thing.'"

"What's with Mark Twain all the time?"

"The Primary People consider Mark Twain America's greatest writer and thinker," said Hercules. "You should read Mark Twain. Start with *Tom Sawyer.*"

"I started that book once. Too many words."

"A problem with most good books," said Hercules.

"Here they come," I said.

One halfie against only eight of them, said Hercules's voice in my head. *Not a fair fight. Try not to hurt anybody.*

The pack approached, spread out, and circled around

me. One of them said, "Hey, loco. You can't walk around here in your underwear." They all laughed.

I remembered I was still wearing only a T-shirt and boxer shorts. I was barefoot.

"I'm a long-distance runner," I said. Good answer. Something Tom would have thought of, if he knew anything about sports. I grinned at them, friendly-like. I didn't feel scared because it seemed like a tryout for a team. Hercules wanted to see what I could do. He wouldn't let anything bad happen to me. Would he?

"Long-distance runner? Barefoot? You goofin' on me?" The first kid looked angry. "Gonna cost you to be here in my park. You gotta pay a admission charge."

All of the guys laughed again.

Remember, said Hercules's voice, *as Mark Twain said, 'Reality can be beaten with enough imagination.'*

I was getting pretty sick of Mark Twain.

The circle around me got tighter. "You deaf?" The kid who had been doing all the talking began slapping his baseball bat into his palm. The others picked up the rhythm. *Smack, smack, smack-smack, smack.*

The circle was so close now, I could hear them breathing along with their smacks. *Hunh, hunh, hunh-hunh, hunh.*

Don't be such a dummy. Imagine something.

What if the baseball bats turned into real bats, flapping their little black wings? But bats weren't really scary. We'd caught some at Scout camp and turned them loose.

Smack-smack, hunh-hunh.

The bats were still baseball bats and they were coming closer.

What if the baseball bats turned into . . . snakes? Just thinking about that made my knees freeze. I was ashamed, a Boy Scout afraid of snakes.

I focused hard on the baseball bats, using my fear to make a terrible picture in my head of wriggling snakes, flashing their fangs.

"Yeeeoow!" One of the kids dropped his bat.

I felt a rush of home-run joy. I focused harder, pouring more fear and energy into my imagination. The fangs started dripping venom!

Kids were screaming, dropping their bats, and running. One kid was crying.

I raised my arms and yelled, "Raiders rule!"

One by one, howling, the guys took off into the trees. Their bats were scattered around me. Plain old baseball bats.

By the time I collapsed into the grass, exhausted, all the guys were gone.

"Not bad," said Hercules, reappearing.

"Not bad? That was the grooviest."

Hercules offered a hand and hoisted me up. "Those were baby steps, making a bunch of wannabe gangsters think their bats were snakes. Your powers are more powerful that that. Eddie, you're not groovy yet. You're just a newbie boobie with a lot to learn."

TEN

WE hugged and jumped and yelled—even Ronnie, who was usually pretty quiet. Alessa cried. Buddy ran around Grandpa's kitchen, licking everybody except Tom, who growled back at him. Eddie and I punched each other's shoulders. In six months, I'd gotten used to Tom again, but now I remembered how much I liked Eddie, a nice, regular guy.

Ronnie looked pale from the trip. Slipping between the Earths is a lousy ride. Galactically speaking, the distance is infinitesimal, but since time as well as space is involved—Eddie's EarthTwo is fifty-four years younger than EarthOne—the trip lasts several hours and beats up your body. You feel as if you're coming down with the flu—headache, chills, nausea, a stuffed nose. The symptoms disappear as soon as you land.

After we quieted down, Grandpa spooned ice cream

into bowls and passed around a plate of cookies. We ate and just sort of looked at one another, grinning. Eddie had borrowed some of Tom's clothes, which were tight on him. When he'd showed up on EarthOne at the landing spot in the woods near the house, he'd been in his underwear. What a great story that was! Grandpa had Eddie, Ronnie, and Buddy hiding in the back of his SUV, under blankets, and he drove into the garage so the drone wouldn't spot them. We pulled the shades in the kitchen and living room.

As usual, Ronnie was wearing clothes big enough for someone twice his size. You'd never think Eddie's little sidekick was the daredevil driver who had helped us escape from the insane asylum the year before by crashing through fences and construction barriers and running over one of Dr. Traum's hologram thugs. Ronnie did it even though his feet couldn't reach the pedals!

Alessa banged a glass on the table. "Okay, guys, what now?" She was in her usual take-charge mode. I had a funny thought: *Ronnie is a little blond boy who looks like a doll and Alessa is a big black girl who acts as if she has all the answers, and they both hide themselves in clothes as big as tents.* I was so into that thought that Alessa had to yell at me.

"Earths to Todd Britzky! Helloooo!"

"It's pretty obvious," I said, stalling for time.

"Obvious that you're brain-dead," said Tom. He can't resist jabbing the needle. Just can't help himself.

"It's obvious that Todd thinks before he speaks," said Eddie. Nice guy. *He* can't help himself.

"We have to give Tom and Eddie a chance to work on their powers," I said. "And Tom has to get a crewcut like Eddie, just in case someone spots him."

"Let Eddie's hair grow in," said Tom.

"We don't have a lot of time," said Grandpa. "And it's very important that no one sees Eddie and Tom together. That's our big secret. Human beings can't know that twin halfies exist." Grandpa sounded serious. "Dr. Traum and the Primary People's Council are meeting. It looks like they've decided that the Earths need to be destroyed before they get a chance to destabilize the universe with extreme weather or nuclear explosion."

"When?" I said.

"The clock is ticking," said Grandpa. "It gets worse. There's a federal agency here on EarthOne, like the one that went after Eddie on EarthTwo, that does nothing but look for aliens. They're the ones who sent the drone. Whatever you decide to do, it has to be soon, before they know too much about us."

"Any ideas?" said Alessa. She was looking at me. We'd been discussing this, but just between us.

"Well, Alessa and I've been talking," I said. "How about what we did last year, Tech Off! Day? Only this time, we'd make it into more than just a day. Like a campaign. Petitions, marches, things like that."

"What's that going to do?" said Ronnie.

"It's an old spy trick," I said. "It's called hiding in plain sight. If everybody is watching us, it will be harder for the government to kidnap us and put us away somewhere. Like they tried to do with Eddie."

Tom gave me a thumbs-up. I was glad he thought it was a good idea. Tom is smart.

"Then what?" said Ronnie.

"People will see kids trying to make things better and they'll want to do it too," said Alessa.

"Meanwhile," I said, "we can figure out how to rescue your dad. And when the aliens and the feds come after us, we'll see who they are, maybe figure out how to take them down."

"Yeah, right," said Ronnie sarcastically. "Like we've been doing."

"So don't come along—stay here," I said.

"Not on this stinking planet," said Ronnie. "You can see the air. The water's dirty."

Eddie held up his hand and Ronnie shut up. Ronnie grabbed Buddy and held the dog on his lap.

"First things first," said Tom. "Eddie and Ronnie need to get phones so we can stay in contact all the time."

Uh-oh. I could see where this was going. "That's tech," I said.

"Duh," said Tom. "This is 2012. How can you have a campaign without communications? Facebook, Twitter, Instagram—all to get the word out. We need to be reading online to keep up with what they're saying about us."

"That would be cheating," said Eddie. "Tech Off! means no tech."

I had a little cold spot in my gut. Nothing was going to work if the twins weren't on the same page.

"Grow up," said Tom. "With the government and the aliens on our tails, we've got to be able to check out, hack in, see what's going on."

"Eddie's right," said Ronnie. "It would be like living a lie, telling people to Tech Off! while we're not."

"Maybe you should go back to 1958," said Tom, "and your rotary phones and TV antennas."

"Let's vote," said Alessa. "I think without our electronics we'd be at a disadvantage, maybe in danger. We wouldn't even know the weather. We could keep the devices out of sight. I vote yes to electronics, with Tom."

Eddie and Ronnie mumbled, "No." They looked defeated.

"Todd?" said Alessa, looking at me triumphantly. "It's two-two. You're the tiebreaker vote."

I could feel the pimples on my forehead light up. She expected me to vote with her and Tom.

"This is a tough one." I tried to look sorry. "Sorry. It would be wrong. I vote no tech."

ELEVEN

IT was hot and stuffy inside the covered wagon. I thought about those pioneer kids stuck in a wagon for months at a time, no tunes or video games. But at least they had chores—the big kids minding the little kids, gathering firewood and starting fires, watching out for Indians, taking care of the horses and oxen and dogs.

I didn't have anything to do. I was keeping out of sight so no one would see me and Eddie together and figure out we were twins. Grandpa had given me a crew-cut like Eddie's. Why did I have to hide on my own planet? They said they could trust Eddie more in public, that I was too much of a loose cannon, but it still made me angry.

It was Britzky who'd spotted the covered wagon outside the restaurant in Nearmont and made the joke that if we were really no tech, we should travel the way Americans traveled 150 years ago. Eddie and Ronnie went nuts—they loved the idea. It reminded them of their favorite TV show, *Wagon Train*. And then Alessa took over. She went to the restaurant—the Westward Ho!—and the owners agreed to lend us the wagon for a couple of days as long as we kept their name on the sides. Nearmont Middle School said we could take a few days off if we kept journals as a special project and spoke at an assembly when we came back. Alessa had a store in town print "Tech Off!" on some black hoodies.

The year before, when Eddie and I had switched places, he was on the *Today* show talking about Tech Off! Day. Now Alessa called up the show and they invited us to come back, but since that had been Eddie being me and now I was me again . . . Argh! It confused even me.

Not that anybody asked me what I thought about all this. I felt as if I was on my own, so I stuffed my cloaking device, grease gun, climate-simulator rods, and modified smartphone into my violin case, along with my violin. The rest of them could have their stupid Tech Off! campaign if they wanted. Not me.

Grandpa attached a hitch to his SUV so he could tow the wagon. Eddie helped him while I stayed hidden in the house. Grandpa backed the wagon into the garage so Ronnie and I could sneak into it without the drone spotting us. We slept in the wagon the night before we left, to try it out. It sucked.

We took off at five thirty in the morning to beat the rush-hour traffic. First stop was Rockefeller Center and the *Today* show. Eddie and Alessa sat on the driver's bench of the wagon, going over what he would say on TV. Britzky sat with Grandpa in the SUV.

I was in the wagon with Ronnie. He also had to hide because how would we explain him? We didn't talk but I could tell he felt useless and uncomfortable too. It was boring and hard to breathe with all the canvas flaps closed. We should have stayed home.

Ronnie stared into space. If I looked at Ronnie, Buddy would growl. At least I didn't have to walk the mutt and pick up after him. Grandpa did that.

We parked near Rockefeller Center while Eddie went to do the *Today* show. Alessa and Britzky went with him. I just crouched in the wagon, making sure my hoodie was up in case someone peeked in.

It seemed like hours before we started moving again.

How you doin', bro? Eddie sounded cheerful. He was happy being the star.

Groovy. I put a sarcastic spin on the word but it went right over Eddie's head.

Neat. Wanna eat?

I wasn't hungry but it was something to do. *Sure.*

Cool. There's a reporter who wants to talk to me. I'm going to ride with her for a while. See you later, alligator.

Britzky climbed into the wagon with white Styrofoam takeout boxes—sandwiches and chips—and bottles of water. Ronnie took his without a word. Buddy tore into his food even as Britzky was opening it.

"Hot in here," said Britzky.

"The pioneers didn't believe in air conditioning," I said.

"They were into conserving energy," said Britzky. A typical not-funny Britzky joke. He was in a good mood.

He climbed out onto the bench where Alessa sat. The SUV started moving and the wagon bounced along behind it. The entire wooden frame shuddered every time we went over a bump or into a pothole. This thing hadn't been built for a twenty-first-century trip. We rattled over a bridge and headed along a river road. The air stank of gas fumes. The sandwich was dry in my mouth. I offered it to Buddy but he turned away. Only time in history a dog refused a sandwich. He really hated me. I drank the water. I tried to sleep.

We stopped at a gas station for a bathroom break. Before I climbed out, I lifted a little flap and peeked through one of the cutouts the pioneers must have used to check for enemies. When I went outside, my hood covered most of my face. There were people along the road waving at us. I would have liked to check out what they were saying about us online, but I didn't want Ronnie to know I had my gear along.

We stopped for the night in the parking lot of a Big-Mart outside Trenton, the capital of New Jersey. Through the flap, I saw a caravan pull in behind us. There were a couple of TV trucks, an ambulance, a half-dozen SUVs, and two black vans sprouting satellite antennas from the roof.

Alessa and Britzky climbed back into the wagon.

"This is so cool," said Alessa. "We just got a call from the governor inviting us to visit him. He's going to proclaim it Tech Off! Week!"

"How did you get a call?" I asked.

She looked embarrassed. "Well, um, we decided we could have one cell, just for travel arrangements and emergencies."

"You have it?" I asked.

"Agent Brown is holding it."

"Agent Brown?"

"The federal-agent guy," said Britzky. "Eddie's bodyguard."

"I thought you were his bodyguard," I said.

Britzky shook his head. "They said a thirteen-year-old kid couldn't do the job."

"Where's Eddie now?" I said.

"He's in a hotel," said Britzky.

"For security reasons," said Alessa.

"What's that mean?" I said. I was getting annoyed. Everybody knew more about what was going on than I did.

Alessa said, "Agent Brown said there had been threats."

"What kind of threats?" said Ronnie. We all turned around, surprised. We'd almost forgotten he was there.

"Agent Brown wouldn't tell us," said Alessa.

"I think he's lying," said Britzky. "I think it's all a government plot to get at the aliens through us. To use us as bait, the way the aliens used us to get your dad."

"Maybe you're paranoid," I said, just so he wouldn't think he knew everything. But maybe he was right. What a mess. I felt sick to my stomach. I had to get out of the wagon and away from all of them. "No one's threatening *me*," I said. I hoped I didn't sound as if I was jealous.

I pulled up my hoodie, grabbed my violin case, climbed over Ronnie and Buddy, and jumped off the back of the wagon.

"Where are you going?" said Britzky.

"Anywhere else," I said.

TWELVE

I<small>T</small> was dark but the Big-Mart parking lot was blazing with light. There were floodlights on poles and the glow of lamps, TVs, and laptops from inside wide-bodied trailers. Kids raced around a playground while their families grilled meat and chicken. Smelled great. Old people sat on lawn chairs, drinking. A geezer noticed my Tech Off! hoodie and waved me over. "You from that wagon?"

Uh-oh. What if he wondered why I looked so much like Eddie? I nodded my head and worked deeper into the hoodie.

He said, "You know Tom?"

"We're real close," I said.

"Some piece of work, that kid. Saw him on TV. Just what we need, people talking face-to-face, no media telling us what to think, no politicians taking our money and telling us what to do."

"Groovy," I said, sarcastically.

"Groovy!" The old man howled with laughter. He turned to his wife at the grill. "You hear that, Susan? They're still saying that." He turned back to me. "Have a burger with us?"

"Thanks. I just ate." The food smelled good but I kept walking. I was still too angry to trust myself not to say the wrong thing. Eddie was relaxing in a hotel while I was stuck in a canvas cage with his brain-dead sidekick and his ratty dog.

Calm down, Tom, I told myself. I was walking behind an old man limping as he dragged a shopping cart, so I imitated his gait. I used to mime-walk on the street in the city just for fun, but I hadn't done it in a long time. The old man turned and said, "Have that leg looked at, sonny—you don't want to end up like me."

I almost felt bad. *No, Tom, you* are *bad,* I reminded myself. I pulled the violin case closer. As soon as I found a safe place, I'd check my devices.

I circled the huge parking lot, walking fast enough to drain off some of my mood. More people offered me food. I took a soda from a family that had a kid my age. He was staring at me. Maybe he recognized me. Kids have better eyesight than old people. I decided to try to get into his mind, see what my powers could do. I concentrated hard, imagining a straw drilling from my head

into his, then sucking out thoughts. I heard—imagined?
—him thinking, *He looks like he plays D&D.*

I wondered if I could put a thought into his head.

I sent back a message: **Prepare to die, gnoll. I am the
prince of drows.**

The kid went bug-eyed and hopped back. I had a
laugh and then I thought, *Is this how you're going to use
your powers, Tom?*

No. I had a better idea. I narrowed my eyesight into
lasers and looked through the wall of an RV. It took
everything I had to penetrate the metal skin.

Bingo!

A fat guy was reading a fishing magazine on the toilet.

Way to save the Earths, Tom.

I found a safe place behind the Big-Mart, a load-
ing platform with just enough light. My violin and bow
were tucked into their protective covers, surrounded by
lumpy cases. I opened the case where I had packed my
cell phone.

Inside was a tin box of hard candies with a note in
Grandpa's handwriting: *Enjoy the treats and use your powers.*

I opened the other cases. They contained extra socks,
little cans of juice, more candy. None of the devices I had
packed were in the violin case.

I was so mad, I thought the top of my head would

pop off. My eyeballs sizzled. What right did Grandpa have to steal my stuff? I heard growling. It was me.

I ran back to Grandpa's SUV. It was empty and locked.

I stood there for a long time, waiting to calm down. I didn't remember ever being so angry.

Finally, I climbed into the wagon. Alessa and Britzky were in their sleeping bags, snoring. I tapped into their brains. They were dreaming. Alessa was dreaming colors, bright floating balloons. Britzky was dreaming shapes, mostly dark rectangles. I couldn't figure out what was going on in Buddy's head, all noise and movement. Ronnie was the toughest to break into. I could feel walls around his thoughts. Finally I heard something: *Gotta get out of here.*

Good riddance, I thought. *Who wants you, creep?*

Then I almost felt bad. Ronnie might be a creepy kid, but that didn't mean he couldn't feel lost and out of it too.

It took me a while to fall asleep. I thought I heard movement in the night, but I ignored it.

Alessa woke me up at dawn.

"What's happening?" I said.

"Ronnie's gone."

THIRTEEN

EDDIE
TRENTON, N.J.
2012

I FELT huge. My head was a balloon bobbing above the world. My arms were long enough to hug the entire audience. *If only Dad could see me now.* Hundreds of faces turned up to me, mouths open, cheering.

Some fat guy in a suit, maybe the governor, was introducing me.

". . . too young to vote but not to lead America: Tom Canty."

There was an explosion of cheering.

I was worried about what to say, but the words just came out of me.

"I see lots of you are holding up your phones and cameras to take pictures, and that's groovy. For now. But tomorrow starts Tech Off! Week, seven days to remember how we used to talk face-to-face and work out problems. Now we'll see if we can still do it before the problems get too big. So tomorrow—no phones, tablets, laptops, not even TV! Can you do it?"

The crowd roared back, "YES!"

Someone took the microphone. He introduced a lady in a suit, who announced that her company was handing out free drinks and chips, brand-new products called Tech Off! Treats in honor of the tour.

I thought, *What tour?*

I heard static, then Tom's voice in my head.

Grandpa and Ronnie are gone.

Where?

They just cut out, Eddie. Grandpa wasn't around last night and Ronnie wasn't in the wagon when I woke up this morning.

Ronnie likes to roam around.

Something's going on, Eddie.

I'm on stage, Tom.

At least look around. You're up high.

I scanned the crowd, looking for Ronnie and Grandpa and imagining where they might be, until I picked up a distant signal, like a blip on a submarine sonar screen in a war movie. The blip was moving away from me. Somehow I felt sure it was Ronnie.

A woman grabbed my arm. "We're moving down the steps now. TV interview." She was talking into her wrist.

I pulled loose. "I've got something to do."

"After the interview," she said, grabbing me again. The agent called Brown rushed up to grab my other arm. I felt like a prisoner.

Tom? I'm picking up a blurry figure. Gray green.

That could be him!

Maybe I'm imagining it.

The powers, Eddie.

"Keep moving," said Agent Brown.

Ronnie's heading into the sun, Tom. That's northwest this time of day.

Let me know if he changes direction. I'm on my way.

FOURTEEN

RONNIE
TRENTON, N.J.
2012

THE only person I'd ever trusted was Eddie, the best guy in the world. That was before he started changing. We'd been on the road for only two days, but already Eddie seemed to think he was some kind of Elvis. He didn't seem like the guy who had protected me in school, shared his lunch, made me his sidekick. Eddie had never asked questions, never asked me why I wore old clothes that hung off me like tents or where my folks were. Or even where I'd been living before he invited me to live with him and his grandpa.

Once, I thought I'd follow Eddie anywhere, do anything he asked, but now I was on this strange planet where I couldn't be independent. I didn't know my way around or where to find food or a safe place to sleep. I was stuck on the wagon. That was what bugged me. I was used to being on my own, in charge of myself. I had needed to get out of that stupid wagon, away from

Eddie's wise-guy twin brother. I had wanted to talk to Eddie before I split, but Eddie had been in the hotel room the night before. And now he was up on stage, surrounded by thousands of screaming people. Like Elvis.

It would just get harder and harder to be with Eddie as the tour went on, I thought. I'd be trapped in the wagon with Tom and his jerky friends, bossy Alessa and know-it-all Britzky. The last time all five of us were together, I'd thought we were almost like a family, but now I could tell that none of them liked me. And they didn't even know me. No one did.

I felt bad about leaving Buddy, but it would be too hard to take care of a dog on the run. Grandpa would be sure Buddy was fed and walked. Eddie wasn't paying any attention to him.

I pushed my way through the crowd, keeping my head deep in my Tech Off! hoodie. Soon as I got a chance, I'd turn it inside out. Grandpa had bought me jeans, T-shirts, and running shoes for the tour. They were stiff and tighter than the clothes I was used to.

"Hey, girly."

A wall of varsity jackets rose up in front of me. Jock jerks. They closed around me, reached for me. I kicked the nearest one's shin, and when he bent over, I karate-chopped his neck. The jock staggered away, leaving an opening, and I slid through it. The crowd closed around the jocks and I turned a corner. When I felt safe enough to stop and look around, I realized I was even farther from Eddie and the stage. Now there would definitely be no chance to talk to him.

Maybe I should go back to the wagon, I thought. No. I couldn't spend another minute with Tom. But I needed to find out what was going on.

All I had were questions.

Who is Hercules?

Is Dr. Traum behind this?

Why is the government involved? On both planets!

Who are friends and who are enemies?

I felt so small, weak, alone.

I felt like crying.

Toughen up, you little sissy, I told myself. *You've been on your own for years; you've been alone since Mom died and Dad disappeared into a bottle and the foster family did bad things and you took off. You didn't need anybody then and you don't need anybody now. Nobody's even looking for you back home. If people were, they wouldn't find you because they're looking for a different person.*

Why did Eddie bring you along to this planet? He felt sorry for you. All he ever cared about was himself, playing the jock star.

C'mon, Ronnie, he did make you feel good, made you feel protected. How much of a friend would Eddie be if he knew the truth about you?

Something warm and wet slapped against my face. Buddy!

I threw my arms around him and buried my face in his soft, furry neck. He cried too.

A hand closed around my arm. "It's okay—I'm a friend," a deep voice said. A big guy with a scraggly red beard and long yellow teeth, dressed in jeans and a New York Yankees warm-up jacket, had me in a grip that tightened as I struggled. I kicked him but he didn't seem to notice. "I'm on your side. Trust me."

"Who are you?"

"My name's Keith. Tom ever mention me?"

"No."

"Maybe he called me Lump."

"Never heard of you," I lied. Eddie had told me about the Lump, the guy who had lived in Tom's house. He was some kind of computer geek who might be working for the government. Eddie liked him because they were both sports fans. Tom hated him.

Keith, or the Lump, smelled bad.

Two men in dark suits with white wires coming out of their ears suddenly surrounded us.

"This one's been on the run from the wagon," said Keith. "Find out what he knows. It's time to take these little punks down."

FIFTEEN

TURNED my hoodie inside out to hide the Tech Off! logo and walked northwest for almost two hours before I began to pick up two moving brain-wave blips that I thought could be Ronnie and a small non-human thing alive enough to be vicious little Buddy. That was all I needed.

They had stopped, probably to rest. I was tired, mostly from the energy I was expending to concentrate on staying on Ronnie's trail. I hoped it would get easier as I got better at it. You really have to work at your powers.

I was hungry but I didn't have any money, so I opened my backpack and took out my violin. I was on a college campus. Last time I fiddled for money had been in a park near a college campus in New York. A college neighborhood is always a good place to play for pay. You get students, teachers, tourists, people who appreciate music and have a little dough. I pulled up my hoodie, opened the backpack in front of me, sat on a bench, and tuned up.

And then I felt sad. The violin was something that Dad and I shared. We played together. We'd warm up with something wild and crazy like the dueling violins from *Riverdance,* which made us laugh, and then we'd go on to Mozart or the Beatles or zydeco, whatever we felt like.

Dad was a famous violin teacher—he traveled constantly to coach big stars before a major concert. Or at least that was what my stepmom and I had thought. Maybe some of it was true. But it was also a cover story so he could do his alien-revolutionary thing. Eddie had a similar cover story for Dad, except he thought our dad was a famous basketball coach who worked privately with pro stars around the world. Eddie and Dad played ball when they hung out.

Sitting in the park with the violin in my hands brought back the old days, before Dad disappeared in what we were told had been a plane crash. We had had a great life, Stepmom and Dad and me, until that had happened. When he disappeared, nearly three years ago, everything had changed, almost overnight. This jerk I called the Lump moved in as a tenant to help pay the bills. I hated him. And I started fighting with everybody.

Teachers called it "acting out." I started getting expelled from schools. Then six months ago all the stuff with the aliens happened, and I found my twin brother. I saw Dad again, just for a minute before he got sucked up by the alien spaceship. The Lump moved out shortly after that, but I still haven't seen my dad since.

"You gonna play or what, kid?"

I almost snapped, "What's it to you, dirtbag," before I realized where I was and what I was doing.

I made myself smile. "What would you like to hear, sir?"

"She likes Mozart." It was a college guy with a girl next to him.

I checked the tuning, then swung into a melody from *The Magic Flute*. The girlfriend clapped and dropped a dollar into my backpack and suddenly I had a crowd. I stuck with Mozart for a while—he was one of Dad's favorites—then did a few Beatles tunes on request. When there was a lull, I did a Willie Nelson song. Old people go nuts when they hear "My Heroes Have Always Been Cowboys" on a violin. Dad used to call that *fiddlin'*.

I was so lost in the music that I was able to forget for a while how things were all messed up and that I was supposed to be chasing Ronnie.

My backpack soon had enough dollar bills for a meal.

I scooped up the money and thanked everybody. They looked sorry to see me go. I was sorry to go too.

I found a diner nearby and ordered a hamburger and fries. There was a TV over the counter. Eddie filled the screen. He was being interviewed. I pulled my hoodie up around my face.

"Last question, Tom. Some people say you've got a political agenda. Some people say you're just trying to sell your sponsors' products. What do you say to all that?"

"I say groovy," said Eddie, with his dopey smile. I could tell he was enjoying himself. "People are talking instead of planting their faces in their iThingies. Just what we want."

Probably still talking about you on their iThingies, dummy.

The newswoman turned to the camera. "And just what America seems to want as the caravan following the Tech Off! tour grows on the road to Washington, D.C.."

Tour? Washington, D.C.? How'd all this happen so fast?

A commercial came on. The waitress said, "Some kid, that Tom. How old do you have to be to be president?"

A few people laughed. I wanted to say, *Forget about age—you have to be born in this America, not in some other planet's America.* I should have felt proud of my brother, but I was annoyed. Not jealous, I thought, just annoyed. Why? Because he seemed to be liking the attention so much. We were supposed to be trying to save the Earths, not having fun.

Do your own job, I thought. *Concentrate on Ronnie.* He wasn't that far away. I finished my food and hit the road.

SIXTEEN

BRITZKY and I sat on the driver's bench of the wagon as the caravan rolled slowly along a two-lane blacktop road. There were farms on both sides. Cows glanced up at us, lost interest, and chewed on. Behind us were dozens of cars, trucks, vans, buses, RVs. The caravan disappeared around bends of the road. How had this happened so fast?

We must have gone viral! But how would I know?

I missed my cell and tablet. Agent Brown let me use his cell while he watched. I wondered how many thousands of Twitter followers I could have by now. Once people knew I was in the wagon, they'd go wild to follow me and also on Facebook, Instagram, Tumblr . . .

"Check this out," said Britzky. He handed me the binoculars. "About twenty cars back."

Two kids our age were standing in the bed of a pickup

truck waving a white bed sheet attached to two broom-
sticks. I focused and read:

Save Earth.

No Nukes.

No Extreme Weather.

"That's so cool. It's what this was supposed to be all
about."

"Enjoy it while it lasts," said Britzky.

"Pessimist."

He pointed up at two drones hovering above the
pickup truck, their propeller blades making the banner flap. "You think the government's going to let this
go on?"

"One banner?"

"One banner leads to another one," said Britzky.
"That's how revolutions happen."

"Revolutions? Shut up. This is just going to be a
week of no texting. That's it."

Britzky lowered his voice. "How do you think the
American Revolution started? Some people didn't want
to pay a tax on tea."

He looked serious. He was making me nervous.

"What do you mean?"

"This isn't some middle-school project, Lessi. Do you
know the Russians have secret files on extraterrestrials?"

"How do you know that?"

"Everything's online if you know where to look."

"So what does that have to do with us?" I said.

"Why do you think these federal agents are on our backs?"

"Why?"

"They're afraid if the Russians or the Chinese get to the aliens first, they'll team up and take over the world."

"But what does that have to do with us?" I asked again.

"The federal agents seem to know the aliens already made contact with us. They think that if they stick with us, they'll find the aliens first."

"Should we warn the aliens? Tell them we're being watched?"

"Are we on Dr. Traum's side?"

"Whose side *are* we on?"

"We better find out, because something big's going to happen."

"Like what? The government is watching us. The aliens are watching us. What are we supposed to do?"

"That's what we have to find out," said Britzky. "And where is everybody?"

Grandpa was missing. Some guy in a black suit with a white wire in his ear was driving the SUV. He wouldn't tell us who he was or where Grandpa had gone. National security, he said.

Ronnie was missing.

Tom was missing.

Even Buddy was missing.

"What can we do?" I said.

"Be ready," said Britzky.

For what? I wondered.

SEVENTEEN

EDDIE
WASHINGTON, D.C.
2012

LIKED seeing myself on TV. I thought I looked good, in shape. And I was getting better at answering questions, especially about Tom Canty. It was easier and easier to pretend to be him. At first, I wanted to be myself—plain old Eddie Tudor, nice guy, jock, leader, Captain Eddie—not a supersmart tech nerd with a mean streak. But as long as nobody was asking about Gargles and Tweeties, I was all right. I practiced reading from the Teleprompter as hard as I practiced free throws. After a while, the lady from the Tech Off! Treats company, Erin, told me it didn't sound as though I were slowly translating from Spanish anymore, not even as if I was reading. She said I was a natural. I started studying videos of myself talking and giving interviews. It reminded me of studying game films. It was just another way to improve. I felt more like myself even while I was pretending to be Tom.

Erin acted as a coach and gave me tips, such as where to put my hands while talking—never in your pockets! —and how to look people in the eye without getting locked in. "And lose the gum!" she'd say. She wanted me to behave more up-to-date, cooler.

One time, she said: "It's sweet that you're an old-fashioned guy, but let's not be so 1950s."

I felt like telling her I *was* from the 1950s, that I came from a planet where cell phones and the Internet and hip-hop hadn't been invented yet, but I didn't.

Erin told me that she and her "people"—she talked to them on the phone a hundred times a day, at least—decided to erase the YouTube clip of me—Tom—greasing that bully in middle school last year. She made it seem like a big deal, as if she were doing me a favor. Big whoop. I liked that little movie of the real Tom in action. It gave me something to copy. Like imitating some great baseball player's batting stance. I wondered what Tom would think about that.

Now that I had an iPad so I could study my own performances, I was starting to enjoy going online. It wasn't so complicated. And the stuff you could see . . .

"You are so coachable," Erin told me more than once.

I wanted to tell her that my real coaches say the same thing, but it would sound like boasting. You have to stay humble or at least act humble. My favorite ballplayers,

Mickey Mantle and Bob Cousy, never hot-dogged it. You never saw them beat their chests after a big basket or show up the pitchers by cakewalking around the bases after a home run. I was seeing a lot of that kind of show-boating on TV these days. I loved ESPN. Twenty-four hours of sports. And they even had a classics channel that sometimes showed ball games from my time, or at least talked about them. I liked the nature channels too, except for the shows about snakes. Being scared of snakes wasn't going to help me make Eagle Scout.

I never expected to be watching so much TV in my hotel room. Erin and the security guys were always hustling me back to the hotel after a speech or an interview. I'd rather hang out and talk to people. I missed Buddy and I missed being on a team, goofing off with a bunch of guys, sharing what was going on, kidding around. I even missed Alessa and Britzky.

And I was worried about Ronnie. When I thought about him, that is.

I was ashamed that I wasn't thinking more about Ronnie. But I knew he could take care of himself. And I had a lot on my mind.

Like making contact with Tom.

Tom, you find Ronnie yet?

They've got him. They keep moving him around. In cars. Just find him.

Maybe you can do better, Eddie.

I'm a prisoner here.

I thought you liked room service.

It's been four days.

Maybe you wanna take over.

Erin's here, Tom. Gotta go.

EIGHTEEN

TOM

SOMEWHERE IN NEW JERSEY

2012

Two tall, vicious-looking dogs glared at me and snarled. Saliva drooled out of their mouths.

I glared back until I remembered reading that you're never supposed to look a dog in the eye unless it's your best friend. It was a good thing these dogs were behind a chainlink fence.

The fence surrounded the scrubby front yard of a dumpy white house on an ordinary street of dumpy white houses with scrubby front yards surrounded by chainlink fences. The only thing different about this particular house was the three shiny black SUVs in the driveway. They looked like the SUVs that cops drive in TV shows.

They had Ronnie inside the house. The blips in my head had gotten stronger as I followed them to the neighborhood and the house. I had stolen a bike — a couple, actually—which makes a huge difference when you're trying to cover a lot of ground. I felt sorry for the bike owners, but this was about the survival of the Earths.

So, now what? Bust in, guns blazing?

There was a Burger Clown down the block with a clear view of the house. I went in, bought some fries, and sat down at a table near the window. It was a table for four people, but it was the only empty table with what TV cops call "a visual." I had to make the fries last because I didn't have any more money. I needed to fiddle for change again, but I hadn't had time while I'd been hot on Ronnie's trail. I'd barely slept in three days.

I stared at the house and tried to concentrate all my thoughts through the Burger Clown window, across the street, and through the dumpy white house's big picture window, which was covered by a curtain.

It was hard to concentrate, because other thoughts kept sneaking in. *What about those dogs? What will I do when I find Ronnie? Where will we go?*

Time to try the powers again.

I concentrated on my brain waves entering the house. Slowly, two gray shapes came into focus, one much smaller than the other. Ronnie and Buddy. There were at least a half-dozen larger shapes. They wouldn't be just regular cops. Federal agents?

I imagined I could hear the cops talking to Ronnie. Gradually, I tuned in voices. They were as unclear as the shapes. They were like gurgles coming up through plumbing.

"Weeheehell you." Could that be *We're here to help you*?

I thought I heard a dog bark. A Buddy-size bark. That set off the two dogs in the yard and drowned out the gurgles.

I tried harder and harder, and just when I thought my head would burst, I tuned in the sounds clearly. Three different rough voices.

"Or the puppy goes to the pound and you go to juvenile hall."

"You'll both be in a world of hurt."

"You might live, not the pooch."

It was exhausting, but a real charge. My powers!

Or was I going nuts?

"C'mon, kid, better say something."

A different voice, closer. "That all you gonna order?"

It took me a moment to pull my brain back into the fast-food joint. A guy in a Burger Clown hat was leaning over my table—a big guy with a red clown nose over his own nose. From his name tag, I saw he was the manager. I was picking up some vibrations that he was upset more than he was angry. I decided not to give him a hard time. I had a job to do.

"It's all the money I have."

"Too bad. People are waiting for this table."

I looked around. It wasn't true. In fact, the place was emptying out. I wanted to say, "They must have tasted your food and gone to McDonald's," but I swallowed that down. *Be cool, Tom. You don't have your grease gun or your climate-simulator rods to back you up.* I could have probably created a little air storm and knocked him on his butt, but then what? I'd have to run for it. Ruin my stakeout.

I tried to get into his mind. It was a mess. He was annoyed at having to wear the red clown nose. He thought he looked stupid. I imagined him thinking, *Is this what I went to school for, to wear this stupid nose and deal with creeps like this little kid?*

Could I really be tuning this in? Or was I just imagining it?

Either way, I felt a little bad for him.

"I'm sorry, sir," I said. I tried hard to look sorry but wasn't sure I was doing it. I didn't feel that sorry. "I'm waiting before my . . . violin lesson."

He glanced at my violin case, and I could sense his mind shifting. So I tried to put a thought into his head: **They make me take the lessons. I hate 'em.**

I imagined his thought: *Give the kid a break. He has problems too.*

"Okay. We get more customers and you gotta move."

"Thanks." I smiled at him.

He smiled back.

I felt a surge of good feelings. We were both happy and I had gotten what I'd wanted. By being nice! That was a strange new feeling for me. But something didn't feel right. And then it hit me: being nice was so Eddie. *You're supposed to be bad,* I told myself. *Hey, man, sometimes being nice can be bad, especially if you're not sincere.*

I focused back on the house across the street. The Burger Clown manager put a soda in front of me but I never got to drink it. I thought I heard Ronnie's high voice screaming.

Across the street, two construction workers in white hardhats and work boots were carrying a long metal pipe. They stopped in front of the house. They heard the screaming too. They looked at each other, then back at the house. They were wondering what to do. I could hear them wondering!

I created a thought and imagined it as a laser beam splitting just before it entered their heads, right through their hardhats.

Throw that javelin through the window and save the screaming kid.

The men hoisted the pipe, turned, and hurled it right at the picture window. It shattered the glass.

The tall, vicious dogs jumped the fence and ran away. The construction workers looked at each other, then ran away too.

By the time I got across the street to the house, Ronnie and Buddy had leaped through the broken window and were racing toward me.

NINETEEN

Eddie!" Ronnie yelled at me. "I knew you'd find me."

"Sorry to disappoint you," I said. "Follow me."

"Oh. Tom." He did sound disappointed.

He followed me around the house to the driveway. I opened the door of the first black SUV. Just as I figured, the keys were under the mat. I had read about this on a secret website for carjackers. Cops want their keys handy for quick getaways but not too handy, such as in the ignition.

"You drive," I told Ronnie. "Like you did when you busted us out of the insane asylum last year."

I ran to the second SUV, found its keys, and pitched them into the bushes. That would block the third car and give us a few extra minutes.

By the time I got back to the first car, guys in suits were running out the door, guns drawn. But Ronnie had the motor running and the police radio on. He was kneeling on the front seat. He still couldn't see over the wheel and reach the pedals at the same time. Buddy was taking up the passenger seat, growling, just daring me to push him off. Ronnie lifted one of his floppy ears and whispered something. The dog gave me a dirty look and went into the back. I climbed in and stomped on the accelerator.

Ronnie blasted through the chainlink fence out to the street and took off.

"Find a highway, and then we'll ditch the car," I shouted. "It probably has a GPS, so it'll be easy to track."

"GPS?"

"Later." I twisted around so I could crawl down under the steering wheel and put my left hand on the brake and my right hand on the accelerator. Just like old times.

Ronnie had really quick reflexes. He maneuvered that big SUV like a racecar, off the street and onto a road that fed into the highway, and then onto the highway with sudden moves, but smooth too, yelling down to me, "Gas . . . more gas . . . let up a little . . . okay, be ready . . . pedal to the metal!"

He didn't call for the brake much, which Grandpa always says is the mark of a good driver, always thinking ahead.

Now *I* had to think ahead. *We ditch the car, but then what? Where do we go? Back to the wagon? Who will protect us there?* I couldn't even get Eddie on the brain waves. *Who do I need to make contact with? The aliens? How do I do that? Am I totally on my own? Just what powers do I have, besides breaking windows? Wind power is pretty awesome but it isn't going to be enough. Hearing voices and thoughts? That would help. But maybe I had just been imagining them. Humans are good at imagining things, even half human.*

Every so often, I popped up to check for police cars, and not just the ones that would be coming after us. How long could we be driving around with a thirteen-year-old boy who looked ten at the wheel? Even if no cops spotted us, what about other drivers? Unless they were all too busy talking or texting to notice Ronnie.

The radio started to crackle. "Enterprise Two, come in, Enterprise Two. This is Federation."

"Gas . . . more . . . okay, we're coming to an exit . . ."

"Enterprise Two, where are you?"

"That doesn't sound like a cop radio," said Ronnie.

"It's got to be a federal task force after the aliens." I felt excited and scared. "Like a special unit. X-Files."

"What?"

"And those call signs: Enterprise and Federation. Pretty cheesy. You'd think they could do better than *Star Trek*."

"What's that?"

"A TV show about looking for aliens. After your time."

"Enterprise Two, you are moving. We have you."

"Okay, Ronnie, off the highway fast. Gotta find, like, an underpass or a concrete building that might block the GPS signal."

I knew he didn't fully understand what I was talking about, but the little guy knew just what to do. Ronnie took a screaming right onto a highway exit, yelling to me, "Gas, gas, all you got . . . okay, lift off the pedal . . ."

I kept poking my head up from under the dashboard, taking quick peeks as we started weaving through side roads toward what looked like an old abandoned industrial park alongside railroad tracks overgrown with weeds.

We circled the area, which was surrounded by a twenty-foot chainlink fence with barbed wire on top.

"Brakes!" The SUV jerked to a stop in front of a gate too heavy to crash through. There was a massive padlock on the front.

I leaned out the window and focused hard, thinking *wind, storm, gale force, cyclone, hurricane, tornado.* The fence was rattling and my head felt as though the padlock banging against the chain links was banging against my skull. But the lock and fence held. I fell back exhausted.

"Can't do it," I whimpered.

Buddy licked my face, hard, to get me going. It didn't feel friendly.

"You can do it," said Ronnie.

I took a deep breath and stuck my head out again. This time I imagined a ray of sunlight shining through a magnifying glass focused on the padlock, imagined the ray narrower and narrower, stronger and stronger, a pencil of light with the heat of a hundred suns, a million suns, burning, scalding out of my brain, boiling me along with the target. The padlock began to sizzle and smoke. Just before I passed out, the padlock melted and the gate swung open.

TWENTY

W E were near Washington, D.C., when Alessa and I were kidnapped off the tour. One minute we were sitting in the wagon eating turkey wraps, and the next we were being hustled toward a van by Erin and two security guys. We didn't have a chance to say goodbye to Eddie, wherever he was. Would Eddie even care?

I tried to squirm out of a security guy's grip. "Where are we going?"

"Someplace else." He pushed me into the back of the van. Alessa was pushed in next to me. There was a metal screen between the front and back of the van. We were in a cage.

Erin leaned in. "It's nothing personal."

Yeah, right, I thought. I said, "Is the tour over?"

"For you two. We're headed for the Capitol."

She slammed the back door shut and locked it. The van began moving.

"Wasn't the tour about kids leading the way?" said Alessa.

"That was then," I said. "Before Homeland Security took over."

"What about Eddie?" said Alessa.

"The good jock? He goes along."

"I thought you liked him."

"I do," I said. "Remember when he was pretending to be Tom last year? He did everything we told him to do. I thought it was because of us. But it's him, the way he is."

"He came up with the idea of Tech Off!" said Alessa.

"Because he couldn't figure out how to turn on a computer."

"What's your point?"

"If you can convince him that something is good for the team, he'll go along," I said. I felt a little disloyal dissing Eddie, but it was the truth. "He's the good jock. He won't ask questions, try to look under the rock."

"And that's bad?"

"It is when there's something under the rock." I suddenly thought, *We could be bugged in here,* and I made the *zip your lip* signal to Alessa.

Alessa got it and shut up too. We looked around for hidden cameras and microphones.

The van was on a highway, then outside a small city, then within rows of suburban homes, and finally into farm country. We turned up a two-lane road, then a one-lane dirt road leading up to a farmhouse surrounded by empty fields as far as I could see.

A man and a woman in dark suits came out of the farmhouse and opened the van doors. The woman said something to the two men in the front seats of the van, then hustled Alessa and me into the house. The van drove off. I could tell that Alessa was getting more scared now. I winked at her, trying to keep a brave front so she wouldn't freak out, but my knees felt like Jell-O.

They put us in separate rooms.

TWENTY-ONE

By the time I came to, Ronnie had driven through the open gate of the industrial park and into an abandoned warehouse, a dingy, rusty old building with high ceilings and a floor littered with scraps of tire rubber and metal shavings. Rats scurried. Were those bats flying up near the ceiling? Buddy leaned out the window and barked at them. I thought I saw a snake slithering through piles of garbage. I shivered.

Ronnie put a hand on my forehead. "Are you okay?"

"Fine," I growled, but I wasn't. I had to hug my elbows to keep my body from shaking. I couldn't tell if it was from thinking about snakes or from using my powers. I hoped using them wouldn't always knock me out.

"That was amazing, the way you melted the lock," said Ronnie. "Can you see through things?"

"Just fuzzy shapes," I said. "I have to practice."

Ronnie frowned.

Then a scary thought elbowed in. "How did they find you?"

"I don't know. I thought I was home free, but then Buddy caught up to me and the agents showed up."

"You didn't take Buddy with you when you took off?"

"He's Eddie's dog."

"Eddie left him," I said. "Eddie said they wouldn't let dogs in the hotel."

We looked at each other but neither of us said anything about Eddie abandoning the rest of us for a hotel room. Neither of us wanted to diss Eddie. Yet.

Ronnie finally said, "I guess after a while, when Eddie didn't come back, Buddy took off after me."

"Why didn't he go after Eddie?"

"Dunno."

"How could he find you?" I said.

"Buddy's a spaniel. He can smell your tracks."

I didn't want to say anything about Ronnie and smells. When I'd first met him and he'd been homeless, you could smell him coming.

Buddy knew we were talking about him. He climbed into the front seat and onto Ronnie's lap. Ronnie lifted one of Buddy's floppy ears and talked to him in a little baby voice.

Ronnie is gay, I suddenly thought. Not that there was anything wrong with that. I believe in equality for everybody, even though you can't trust most people. I wondered if Eddie knew.

After a while, I said, "We can't stay here. There are tracking devices in the car. The warehouse walls may not be enough to block them." I started ripping out all the dashboard wires. One of them had to be the GPS.

"I need to ask you," said Ronnie in a low voice. "Can you see through clothes?"

"I haven't tried." That was true. I hadn't had time. I remembered the guy on the toilet in the trailer. I hadn't looked through his *clothes*. "But I think so. Why?"

Ronnie's mouth twisted as if he was trying to say something and couldn't figure out how to form the words. He kept stroking Buddy, nervously, harder and deeper, until Buddy started to squirm.

"Hey, what's this?"

Ronnie grabbed one of my hands and guided it to a spot on Buddy's back, near his neck, where the fur and flesh were thick. I felt something solid, pea-size.

I fingered it, and when Buddy didn't seem to notice, I squeezed it hard. Buddy still didn't react. It wasn't part of his body.

"Must be a microchip pet finder," I said. "People implant it right under the fur, and then if the pet goes missing, they can track it. It's a kind of GPS."

"GPS? When are you going to tell me what that means?"

"It's an electronic tracking device. I bet somebody used it to find you."

"That makes no sense," said Ronnie. "I don't think we have microchips on our planet yet."

"They could have put it in Buddy here on the tour. Maybe that security guy Brown. Takes a minute to inject it. They probably figured Buddy would always be with Eddie. It was a way to keep track of him."

"What are we going to do?" said Ronnie.

"Leave him here, tied up so he can't follow us," I said.

Ronnie's eyes actually bugged out. His mouth dropped open. "Can't do that. It's Buddy."

"You want to get caught again? What were they doing to you when you were screaming like a girl?"

Ronnie sucked air. "I'm not leaving Buddy. You're so smart, Tom—figure something out."

TWENTY-TWO

My room had a narrow bed, two wooden chairs, and a chest of drawers. No window. There were two framed needlepoints on the wall. One read HOME IS WHERE THE HEART IS. The other read THE ROAD TO A FRIEND'S HOUSE IS NEVER LONG.

The signs made me lonely and sad. I sat down on the bed and cried for a minute or two, then stood up. *Pull yourself together, Lessi. It's always darkest before the dawn.* Now, that was a needlepoint for you!

There was a knock on the door. Before I could say, "Come in," the door banged open. The woman in the dark suit marched in, slammed the door behind her, and sat down in one of the wooden chairs.

"Sit down," she said.

I kept standing. I didn't feel so small and weak when I was taller than her.

"Whatever. I'm Agent Mathison and you are in big trouble, young lady."

I sat down.

"Here's the deal. We know everything. Your pal Todd just spilled his guts, which confirmed what we already knew. He won't be prosecuted. But you will be prosecuted and so will your parents. Prison time. Unless you cooperate."

"How?"

"Tell us what you know."

"About what?"

"About Tom."

"What about him?" I felt confused. Tom as Tom, or Tom as Eddie, or Eddie pretending to be Tom? I almost asked Agent Mathison, then bit my tongue to shut myself up. Just what was it Agent Mathison knew?

"When did you first meet Tom?"

Be cool. Tell the truth as much you can. "Last year when he started Nearmont Middle School. We were both in orchestra. I played cello and he—"

"Who had the idea of Tech Off! Day?"

It had been Eddie being Tom, I thought, but something warned me against saying too much right away. I didn't believe that "Todd just spilled his guts." That wasn't Britzky. "It was Tom's idea. He thought people really needed to talk to one another face to—"

"What about the voices?"

I went into dumb mode. It worked with Mom and Dad when they interrogated me. "Voices?" I thought she was talking about the voices Tom hears, which he had thought were imaginary but now knew belong to Eddie and to aliens, like his dad and Dr. Traum.

"Telling him what to do."

"Tom never lets people tell him what to do."

"You think you can play dumb with me, young lady?" Agent Mathison was scowling.

"Is Tom in trouble?"

"Worry about yourself. You're the one in trouble for withholding information from a federal officer."

"Like FBI?"

"FBI takes orders from us."

"I haven't really seen much of Tom lately." That was true. True was good when you were playing cat and mouse. "He's, like, off the wagon a lot."

"Where does he go?"

"I don't know. Erin says he's getting ready for his interviews."

"I'm losing patience. What about the aliens?"

"You mean like illegal . . ."

"Now I'm getting angry."

"Aliens from other planets?" I made the face Mom hates, the gimme-a-break face.

"Don't play with me."

I wondered how much Agent Mathison knew about the aliens. Obviously, she didn't know Tom was a half alien or a twin. Had to keep it that way. What about Britzky? If he spilled his guts and I didn't . . .

"Do you think Tom is crazy?" said Agent Mathison.

"No. Why?"

"We know about the voices he hears. And talks to. We think you know about them."

"I don't." I tried to put a lot of sincerity into my voice. Probably a mistake when you're lying.

Agent Mathison stood up. "I'll let you think about it. I hope you're not hungry."

She marched out. As I heard the door lock, I realized I was very hungry.

TWENTY-THREE

T HE room had a narrow bed, two wooden chairs, and a chest of drawers. No window. There were needlepoints on the wall. THERE'S NO PLACE LIKE HOME and MY HOUSE IS YOUR HOUSE.

Pretty obvious attempt at a psych-out, I thought. Trying to make me lonely and afraid. They didn't know who they were dealing with. I jammed a chair under the doorknob. I thought about Lessi. Hoped she was okay.

When the knock came, I said, "Who's there?"

A jolly voice said, "Room service."

"Sorry, I'm busy."

The voice laughed and rattled the doorknob. "The old chair-under-the-doorknob trick. Pretty good, but these warm cookies are getting cold."

I could smell them. These guys could break down the door if they wanted to—no point in being unfriendly

until I had to. Might as well open the door. A few cookies weren't going to crack me.

"Hey, man, sorry about all this." The man in the
dark suit was carrying a tray with cookies and soda. "I'm
Agent Quinn. We were concerned about your safety
back there, had to move quickly to get you out." He put
the tray on the chest of drawers. "Help yourself."

He sat down in one of the chairs. He had a tough face
but he was smiling.

I could feel my heart beating, but I stayed cool. I took
a cookie. "Our safety?"

"After they kidnapped Ronnie, we figured they'd
come after you."

"Who kidnapped Ronnie?" It didn't make sense.
Ronnie had taken off because he couldn't stand the real
Tom and what Eddie had turned into. He couldn't stand
being cooped up in the wagon with me and Alessa.
Strange little guy.

"Wish we knew. Maybe you can help us. Who's Tom
been talking to?"

"We don't see him that much. He has interviews
all day."

"What about before you started the tour? Anything
strange?"

Got to see where this is going, I thought. *Tell him stuff he probably knows*. "The fight in the cafeteria? The kid they called Hercules?"

Agent Quinn nodded. "Heard about it. Don't kids fight all the time? What was so special about that fight?"

Uh-oh. Did I trip myself up? Is this guy trying to get me to talk about aliens?

"Tom had a rep," I said. "You ever see the YouTube clip where he greased a bully in his last middle school?"

Agent Quinn looked interested. "How'd we miss that? Good intel, Todd. So what's your theory?"

"When this Hercules came to school, he heard about Tom. He was like a gunfighter who shows up in a new town and right away has to prove himself."

"I love Westerns," said Agent Quinn. "You see *Cowboys & Aliens*?"

Now, that was smooth. This guy was no lunkhead. But neither was I.

"Yeah. I don't believe in aliens, so it kind of spoiled a good Western."

"What if I told you there really are aliens and we need your help to track them down before they attack Earth?"

"Really?" I hoped I didn't overdo my fake expression of amazement.

"You're sharp, Todd, the kind of kid who grows up to be an agent."

I figured he was just buttering me up, but he wasn't off base. I'd thought about going into law enforcement.

"I was like you when I was your age, Todd, but of course, I wasn't in the trouble you're in."

"Trouble for what?"

"Lying to a federal agent, to the government. We want to give you the same chance we gave Alessa to come clean and avoid charges and prison time."

"Come clean about what?" I tried to keep my voice steady.

"About the aliens that Tom is in contact with." Agent Quinn stood up. "Enjoy your snack, Todd. Try to remember anything to help your situation."

"My situation?"

"Nobody knows where you are, Todd. We could keep you here forever."

He locked the door behind him.

TWENTY-FOUR

THE first time I thought about busting loose, I was watching myself on TV being Tom and I was saying, "Whatever happened to responsibility, loyalty, obedience, reverence? Staying strong as a country, protecting ourselves?" I had been reading that off the Teleprompter.

I believe in all that—I am a Scout!—but I don't really talk like that.

Then the TV showed some old guys in suits and ties sitting around a table talking. One of them said, "A child has come to lead us," and another said, "He's a puppet of dangerous interests," and another said, "He's a boy genius," and another said, "He's a holy fool."

I knew they were talking about me—at least, the kid they'd seen on TV, who wasn't really me.

My mind was spinning like after getting sacked hard in a football game.

That was when I finally clicked off the TV and tried to think. The television was always on when I was in the hotel room, and I was in the room most of the time, watching TV and eating room-service food. I hadn't felt like a prisoner at first. I could choose anything I wanted from the room-service menu. I loved ordering burgers, fries, shrimp cocktails, ice cream, soda. When I noticed I was softening up and slowing down from all that food, I started doing pushups, sit-ups, stretches. It was a big room. I felt better.

I could exercise while I watched TV. It was hard not to watch. The shows were amazing—the movies you could click on, the language, the girls, the music, the action, things blowing up in slow motion, all that blood—how could they get away with it? I'd never seen anything like that on EarthTwo. I liked the cop shows best. They were easy to follow even while I worked out.

But I couldn't leave the room on my own. I'd been angry when I'd discovered that. One afternoon when I'd felt bored and lonely, I decided to go down to the lobby, just to hang out and see what was going on. When I stepped out of my room, I spotted two Agent Brown types in the hall, one in a chair near my door, the other down by the elevators. They both jumped up and blocked my way. They were polite. Orders, they'd said. There were too many people who wanted to meet me. Some of them might want to hurt me.

Later, Erin explained that I was getting to be too famous to go around like an everyday guy.

That was when I remembered busting out of the hotel room less than a week ago on EarthTwo, making the TV explode and running down to the lobby in my underwear. I could do that again. Would Hercules be waiting for me downstairs in a taxi the way he'd been last time? Where *was* Hercules? I could probably escape without him. But then what? Where were Tom and Ronnie and Buddy?

I tried to focus but I couldn't tune Tom in. I concentrated until my head was splitting, but it felt as though something was blocking the transmission. Where was Tom now? I had to get out of there. I needed to talk to Tom, be with him. Two halfie twins could figure this out. Two halfies make a whole.

TWENTY-FIVE

TOM
SOMEWHERE IN NEW JERSEY
2012

'M no touchy-feely guy, but I had to feel sorry for the panic on Ronnie's face, even though I couldn't understand making such a big deal over a dirty little dog.

"We've got to leave him," I said.

Ronnie clenched his jaw. "Not going to happen."

"He'll lead them right to us."

"You can take off if you want."

"I will. I'm Tom, not Eddie. I don't care about you or your dog."

"If you're Tom," said Ronnie, looking me right in the eye, "then do something. You're supposed to be so smart."

That got to me. I was the twin who was supposed to figure things out. And maybe I did care just a little. I didn't really want to leave them.

"As long as that chip is in him, he'll—"

"So get it out," said Ronnie. His face was hard.

"Yeah, sure, find a vet, convince him to do it and not tell anybody. You serious?"

"I'm serious about not leaving him." There was no question Ronnie was serious.

Now what?

I probed Ronnie's mind. There were walls and angles, but I got to a clear place. *Tom acts mean but he really cares. Tom's smart. Tom can help us.*

Better believe it, I thought. But then I wondered, was my imagination making up those thoughts? Or maybe Ronnie created those feelings to trick me?

Man, you don't trust anybody.

I said out loud, "Must be a first-aid kit in the car."

Ronnie was swift. "You think we can do it?"

"We have to."

He gave me a big smile.

The first-aid kit was a metal suitcase packed with enough equipment and medicine to treat a major wound. We'd stolen the car of some prime-time cops. We unrolled a silvery survival blanket on the filthy floor. I'd read about field medicine on a survival website. I took out what I thought we would need: lots of sterile gauze pads, scalpels in their paper packages, needle and thread, tweezers, scissors, and antiseptic. I didn't know what the antibiotics and painkillers would do to a dog, so I left them in the suitcase.

Ronnie led Buddy to the blanket, gently pushed him down, and held him in place. Buddy let him—he trusted him. Ronnie lifted Buddy's ear and began whispering into it. They both looked nervous.

I pretended I wasn't. I tried to sound like a surgeon on a TV show. "We'll have that right out, old Buddy-roo."

"Eddie always says that you want Tom on your team when the going gets tough."

"He really says that?"

"Yeah. He also says you aren't always so nice."

We both laughed.

I picked up a scalpel and imagined cutting into Buddy, the blood shooting out, the dog screaming in pain.

I said, "Maybe *you* should . . ."

Ronnie nodded and picked up the sharp little scissors. He cut away as much of Buddy's hair as he could around the microchip, leaving a bald patch. I soaked that with antiseptic. I handed Ronnie the scalpel and poured antiseptic on the blade.

Ronnie was very slow and careful, cutting a tiny semicircle around the little lump. Buddy grunted but he stayed still. He yelped once when Ronnie squeezed the cut and a gray metal button popped right out of his fur.

There was hardly any blood. I poured more antiseptic on the cut and Ronnie covered it with a bandage. Buddy whimpered.

"Good dog," I said.

Buddy looked up at me, sneezed, then stood up and shook himself off. He growled at me.

"Back to normal," I said. "That was great, Ronnie."

Ronnie let out a long breath.

I picked up the microchip off the silver blanket. I could feel indentations on the casing. I cleaned off the chip and studied it. There were letters and numbers: NASA—205BA46—000DI.

"Government, all right," I said. "The space agency is hoping Buddy will lead them to the aliens through us."

"What now?"

"We've got to get out of here. Look for a sewer drain we can drop the chip down on the way out."

"Where are we going?"

I shook my head. "I guess we just start running."

"There was another guy with the ones who grabbed me—he was different," said Ronnie.

I had a queasy feeling. My psychic powers? "Red whiskers?" I asked.

"How'd you know?"

"The Lump," I said.

"He told me that. Eddie mentioned him once. Who exactly is he?"

"Big trouble," I said. "Right after Dad disappeared a few years ago, he moved into our house. Mom said he was just a tenant, helping with the mortgage, but I thought he was her boyfriend by the way he ordered her around, and that got me mad."

"No wonder you always seemed like such an angry guy," said Ronnie. "When you came to EarthTwo pretending to be Eddie, I thought you were Eddie gone nuts."

"The Lump acted like some kind of government agent, always down in the basement on his computers. Hacking, I thought. He'd come up for a beer, sprawl all over the couch, hog the TV."

"Eddie said he liked him," said Ronnie. "They watched baseball together."

"Eddie *would* like him," I growled. Buddy growled back.

But then Buddy jumped away from Ronnie and cocked his head up. It took a moment, but then we heard the humming sound too. Drones.

"I think we need to split up," said Ronnie.

"Why?"

"You'll have a better chance without us slowing you

down," he said. "If they find you, they'll know you and Eddie are twins, that there are two of you. That would be bad."

I hadn't thought of that. Ronnie was right. Still . . .

"I think we should stick together," I said.

Ronnie shook his head. "Maybe you can hide somewhere here. I'll keep the microchip and be out in the open. Once they've got me, they won't keep looking for you. They don't know you exist."

"What about you?"

"I'll be okay."

"You weren't okay the last time they got you."

"You saved me," said Ronnie. "You'll do it again."

TWENTY-SIX

'D never really been hungry before, not the kind of *hungry* hungry where your stomach hurts and growls and your eyeballs feel loose and your brain feels light and floaty. In fact, I've rarely missed meals. I've always been heavy, and my parents have tried every kind of diet that might slim me down. I learned from the No-Diet Workshop that you should never eat on a totally empty stomach because then you'll eat too much. You should always carry something to eat—carrot sticks or even an energy bar. But I didn't have anything now.

I wondered why I wasn't more scared than hungry, but it was hard to be too scared when I was so hungry. Hunger beat fear. Anyway, weren't federal agents supposed to be on *our* side?

I was worried about Britzky. I knew Agent Mathison had been lying when she'd said Todd had spilled his guts to save himself. He would never do that. He was crazy brave. But maybe they'd tortured him. Maybe they knew enough to get him to say something that tripped him up.

What were we hiding? A lot. That Tom has a twin, Eddie. That they are half human beings, half aliens. That there are aliens out there who created a second Earth —fifty-four years behind this one—and are now considering destroying both of them because they are worried that we earthlings aren't being responsible in terms of nuclear weapons and extreme weather. We don't trust the aliens, but we had to cooperate with them if we wanted to get Tom and Eddie's dad back.

Maybe the federal agents would want to stop the aliens from destroying both Earths too, if they knew about the Earths. Wasn't that a good thing? Maybe we should be cooperating with them.

I'm so hungry.

Stay strong, Lessi.

I remembered another tip from the No-Diet Workshop. *Think of the food you want most, imagine covering it with something horrible, and you will be free of all craving.*

I imagined double-cheese pepperoni pizza.

I imagined Buddy peeing, then pooping, on it.

My hunger disappeared. I felt as if I had just had a huge meal and felt sick.

It worked!

The door opened and Agent Mathison walked

in. She was smiling. "How about something to eat, Alessa?"

The hunger whooshed back.

"Double-cheese pizza with pepperoni?" I said. The words just slid out, like pizza out of an oven.

"Whatever you'd like. After you answer a couple of questions."

I tried to bring back the picture of the poopy pepperoni. It wasn't working.

"We need to find Tom and we need to find him fast," said Agent Mathison. Her face was hard again. "Millions of lives are at stake. Do you want to be responsible for millions of lives?"

I shook my head.

"Didn't think so. When was the last time you saw Tom?"

"On TV?"

Agent Mathison sat backwards on one of the chairs and tilted it toward me. As her face came closer and closer, it looked more and more like a hatchet. "Last chance, Alessa. When was the last time you saw Tom?"

That was when I made the big mistake. "When he took off after Ronnie?"

"When was that?"

I thought hard. "Yesterday? The day before?" I had lost track of time.

Agent Mathison looked at her notebook. "Did Tom come right back?"

"No."

"How did he give his speech that afternoon?"

It was Eddie who had given the speech. *OMG.* I was suddenly more scared than hungry. "I don't know."

"Can't be two places at the same time, can you?"

"No."

"So you must be lying." She was pushing her sharp face closer to mine again.

"I'm not."

"Then explain how you saw Tom give his speech but you know he didn't come back from chasing after Ronnie." Agent Mathison stood up fast and let her chair clatter across the floor.

I felt panicky. *Cool down, Lessi. Take deep breaths.*

"I guess he came back and I didn't see him."

"You're lying, Alessa, and millions of people are going to die because you're lying."

It could be true. If the aliens blew up the Earths, millions—no, billions—of people would die. I felt hungry and scared *and* confused. Whose side were we on?

TWENTY-SEVEN

AGENT Quinn had left all the lights on and turned some awful music on full blast. I couldn't doze with the lights so bright and the music ricocheting off the walls. I didn't even recognize the music, it was so loud. It made my head feel like a punching bag. A little nap was all I needed so I could think.

I kept chanting, *Be strong.* I'd read that prisoners of war did that to keep their spirits up. I knew what the agents were doing to me. Depriving a person of sleep is the most effective torture of all.

I had no idea how much time had passed before Agent Quinn came back into the room with a woman who was also wearing a dark suit and a white shirt, but no tie.

Agent Quinn turned down the sound. "This is Agent Mathison, Todd. She's been talking to Alessa."

"She okay?" I said.

"She's taking care of herself," said Agent Mathison.

She had a nasty edge to her voice that reminded me of the serrated blade of a bread knife. I'd cut myself once with a bread knife. Stitches. I tried to use the memory of the pain to cut through my fogginess.

"You paying attention?" said Agent Quinn.

I wasn't. I was drifting away, my mind bobbing in the sleepless sea.

"You better start taking care of yourself, Todd," said Agent Mathison. "She told us all about Tom."

"What about Tom?"

"I'm asking the questions," snapped Agent Mathison. "When was the last time you saw him?"

"When he took off after Ronnie."

"Did you see him when he came back?"

"He didn't come back. At least not before you kidnapped us."

"It's not a kidnap when federal officers detain you," said Agent Quinn.

"What kind of federal officers?"

"No time for that. Millions could die."

"Die? How?"

Agent Mathison turned to Agent Quinn. "Turn up the sound and let's get out of here. Far as I'm concerned, he's a terrorist and can stay in this room until his head explodes."

"I understand your feelings, Agent Mathison," said

Agent Quinn, "but Todd is a good person who wants to do the right thing. Let's give him a chance."

Good cop, bad cop. *How old is that?* I thought. But I was glad Agent Quinn was in the room. Agent Mathison scared me.

"Okay," she said. "One chance." She turned her sharp face back to me. "Is Tom an alien?"

Don't lie; don't tell the truth. How did you do that?

"No," I said. He's a half alien. So I wasn't technically lying.

"I'm done here," said Agent Mathison. "You can baby-sit him if you like, but he's no good to us."

"Then let me go." I hated the whine in my voice.

"Too late for that," said Agent Mathison.

Agent Quinn looked unhappy. As he followed Agent Mathison out the door, he cranked up the sound.

TWENTY-EIGHT

KEITH—the Lump—walked into the warehouse alone.

"Hiya, Ronnie." I wondered how he knew my name, then remembered being questioned by the agents. That was about all they found out—my name. And Buddy's.

"Hey, Buddy." Keith waved a greasy bag of McDonald's food in one hand and a bag of dog treats in the other. I had to hold Buddy by the collar to keep him from running over to Keith.

Behind Keith, through the open door, I could see the agents.

Keith had one of those friendly, ugly faces that made you want to like him. He was big and his plaid shirt and jeans were wrinkled. There were tiny bits of food in his red beard. I could see why Tom called him the Lump.

He set the McDonald's bag down next to me. "May I give Buddy a treat?"

I nodded. He held out a cookie shaped like a cat. Buddy took it gently and Keith patted his head.

"So, where is he?"

"Who?" *I've got to stall as long as I can,* I thought, *so Tom can figure out how to get away.*

"For his sake, Ronnie, tell me where he is. You know what those agents are like. The guys outside want to tear-gas the place. I don't want Tom to get hurt."

"Since when?"

"I've always liked him. He was the one who didn't like me. He thought I was his stepmom's boyfriend."

"You weren't?"

"I was just a tenant, helping her pay the mortgage after her husband died." He smiled at me. His teeth were yellow and crooked.

"That's not true, Keith."

"You're pretty smart, Ronnie." He got so close that I could smell french fries on his breath. He was looking at me so carefully, I got nervous.

"You're some kind of cop."

"True. I work for a federal agency that searches for extraterrestrial life. I monitor interplanetary chatter. I was in Tom's house because I knew he was in contact with another planet."

"Really? Tom?" I pretended to be surprised. *I've got to keep him talking,* I thought. I remembered that Eddie had liked Keith. They had watched baseball together. "Tom said he watched baseball with you."

"He remembered that? Yeah, it was a good time. He seemed different."

No kidding, Sherlock. That had been Eddie, not Tom. "Like how?"

Keith pushed his red whiskers even closer. "You ever get the feeling he's two different people?"

"Like a split personality?"

"Exactly."

I heard a voice in my head that sounded like Tom's. ***Don't let him know we're twins.***

When I nodded at Keith, I almost brushed his whiskers because he was leaning in so close. "I heard he had to take some pills for his behavior. Maybe that made him act different."

Keith pulled back and scratched his whiskers. "That might do it. By the way, where did you hear that?"

I felt a fluttering in my stomach. Uh-oh. Had to be careful here. "I don't know."

"Kids in school?"

"Could be."

"How could that be, Ronnie? You never went to Tom's school."

I just shrugged.

"So who are you, Ronnie? While we had you, we ran your prints and pictures. It's like you don't exist on this planet."

When you're lying, it always helps to tell a little bit of the truth. "I'm a runaway. Homeless."

Keith smiled. "Even a homeless kid leaves some kind of footprint on his planet."

Tom's voice again in my head. *Careful. He's closing in.*

I liked the idea that Tom was still looking out for me.

"How'd you smash those windows and escape?" said Keith.

"What do you think?" Still stalling. It wasn't the coolest thing to say.

"I think whoever we're looking for sent you down to make contact with Tom. But why?"

I shrugged.

I'm coming back, I heard in my mind. *You can't face this alone.*

"We need to find that out, Ronnie. By any means possible."

I felt chilled. Eventually, they were going to find out the truth about everything. I started to panic.

"Where is Tom?" Keith asked again.

"Right behind you, Lump," said Tom.

Keith smiled and turned around. "As expected, the hero returns."

TWENTY-NINE

I FELT like a prisoner. It was my own fault. I had let it happen. I remembered when Hercules had said that my elevator didn't go to the top floor. It had stung, but then I'd flushed it out of my head, like the memory of an intercepted pass. Coach always says you can't dwell on the negative because that will drag you down.

Coach says. Coach says. It was always *somebody else says,* somebody else telling me what to do. Coach. Dad. Grandpa. Tom. Erin. I had thought it was a good thing to be coachable, good that I listened to people and let them help me improve. Wasn't it? A lot of players insist on doing things their way, and most of the time they don't improve on their own. They drop off the team.

Tom isn't coachable—he's always talking back, questioning, doing everything his way as though he knows better. Maybe he does know better. At least he isn't a puppet.

What would Tom do in my place now?

What a joke. *They think you're Tom, but they want you to act like Eddie. You want to act like Tom, but you're still Eddie.* Maybe it was time to be the Eddie whose elevator goes to the top.

When Erin showed up that morning to take me to an interview, I told her I wanted to see Grandpa and my friends.

She sighed and shook her head. "It's not a good time to hang out at the wagon."

"Why can't they come visit me here?"

"They all went home. They were uncomfortable in the wagon."

"So get them hotel rooms too," I said.

Erin sighed more deeply. "I hate to tell you this," she said, "but they're jealous of you getting all the attention."

"So let them come on stage with me. I'd like that."

"The truth is," said Erin, "they were homesick and bored of the tour. They wanted to get back to school, to their lives. They really weren't committed to the tour."

Too many different answers. I wondered what was true. I wished I could look into her mind.

Could I? I stared at Erin's forehead as if I were looking for a hole between blitzing linebackers. Nothing. I remembered a TV show where the cops slipped a skinny wire with a tiny TV camera at its tip under a door and got to see what was going on in the bad guy's room.

I imagined slipping a tiny microphone up Erin's nose and into her brain.

I heard static!

And then, *This nimbot is getting to be a pain. Where is Keith?*

Her phone rang and she turned away. "There you are. We're ready . . . That long?"

She turned back to me and gave me a phony smile. "Someone's coming—an old friend of yours."

Keith? The guy Tom called the Lump! Tom thought he might be some kind of government agent—when the Lump had been living in Tom's house, he'd always been working on computers in the basement. I'd gotten along with him because we were both Yankees fans, but if he came here, he might figure out that there are two of us.

"Old friend? Groovy," I said. I made myself smile at Erin. "Who?"

"A surprise."

I could blow up the TV like I had done back on EarthTwo, bust out of the room and try to escape, but there were all those Browns out there and everyone knew who I was. I needed Hercules. But I was on my own.

I got the microphone back up her nose. This time, I tried to push a thought into her mind. *Erin is sooo nice.*

She smiled at me. I thought I heard *So sweet and pathetically dumb.*

Think so? I'm sooo hungry.

"You look hungry. Want something while we're waiting?"

"Like you were reading my mind, Erin."

She picked up the phone and ordered a hamburger, fries, and soda. I was sick of that stuff, but I just nodded and smiled harder.

When the knock and the call of "Room service!" came, Erin was texting and didn't seem to notice. One of the Browns opened the door so a waiter could push his cart into the room.

I imagined sticking a straw into the Brown's ear and whispering, *Waiter's got a gun.*

"GUN!" yelled the Brown, just like in the cop shows.

He tackled the waiter. The cart rolled across the room into Erin.

I opened the hotel room door wider and yelled, "GUN!"

As the Browns in the hall rushed into the room, I jumped out, slammed the door, raced to the stairway, and plunged down the steps.

In the lobby, I imagined a fog so thick that no one could see me. I walked through it, bumping into people, saying I was sorry, until I went through the hotel's revolving doors.

The fog didn't follow me outside. I was on the sidewalk. People were waving at me. "Way to go, Tom . . . We love you, Tom . . ."

"Stop right there, Tom!" Browns were pouring out the revolving door behind me.

More were coming at me from across the street. I was trapped.

Then I heard a familiar voice.

Hop on, Eddie.

THIRTY

ALESSA
SOMEWHERE IN NORTHERN VIRGINIA
2012

T AKE your clothes off," said Agent Mathison.

"What?" I wasn't sure what I had heard.

"You heard me."

I didn't want to hear it. My mind turned off. My ears filled with static.

"Strip!" The word cut through the static.

No way, I thought. *You can kill me.*

"I'll do it myself, then." Agent Mathison pushed up the sleeves of her black suit jacket.

Don't care what you do. Not going to happen. I wrapped my arms around myself. I was wearing jeans and a black Tech Off! hoodie over a black Tech Off! T-shirt. I always try to wear black. I think it makes me look thinner.

"You want me to call Agent Quinn in here to help me take your clothes off?"

I imagined the two agents ripping my clothes off. As

hard as I struggled, I'd be no match for the two of them. Both bigger and stronger. Probably trained to do this. The thought of Agent Quinn seeing me naked sent an icicle down my back.

Agent Mathison opened the door and waved Agent Quinn in. He'd been standing right outside, waiting.

"We need to make sure you aren't packing anything, Alessa," said Agent Quinn.

Agent Mathison cackled. "Can't imagine what she could hide under all that flab."

In a kindly voice, Agent Quinn said, "It's routine, Alessa."

I took a deep breath. "If it's so routine, how come you didn't do it right off?"

"We thought you'd be cooperative," said Agent Quinn. "We didn't think we'd have to treat you like a suspect."

"Suspect of what?"

"No time for your questions," said Agent Mathison. "Take. Off. Your. Clothes."

I didn't move. Couldn't move. I was frozen. I already felt naked. There was water in my eyes. *Don't cry, Lessi. Hang in there.*

"I'm losing patience," said Agent Mathison, tapping the toe of her black boot.

"Maybe we need a little more understanding here," said Agent Quinn. "It's not that Alessa is being unpatriotic or criminal. She's hung up on body-image issues."

Good cop.

"She's just fat," said Agent Mathison.

Bad cop.

"She's not totally comfortable in her skin," said Agent Quinn.

Good cop.

"There's so much of it," said Agent Mathison.

Bad cop.

Go ahead, I thought. *You think I haven't heard all of this before?*

"Her feelings make her do things against her better nature," said Agent Quinn. "Such as protecting Tom."

"Being a tub of lard is no excuse for endangering the nation," said Agent Mathison. "And the jury won't think so either."

I was cold and hot. I sucked for breath. The arms I had wrapped around myself were the only things keeping me from falling apart. My fingers dug into my rolls of flesh. *Stay tough. If they keep you here and starve you, Lessi, you'll wake up skinny.*

If you come out alive.

"Maybe she's hiding information about Tom in all

that blubber," said Agent Mathison. "A thumb drive, notes—who knows? We better check."

"I'm afraid you're right," said Agent Quinn. "But how about one more chance. I know she wants to do the right thing."

"Okay," said Agent Mathison. "Explain this, Alessa. You say Tom didn't come back after going after Ronnie. But you say you saw him give his speech. How's that possible?"

"I don't know."

"She doesn't want to tell us," said Agent Quinn.

"Let her starve!" screamed Agent Mathison. She turned away.

"Wait." It just came out of me. "There are two of them. They're twins."

"No wonder we didn't have a fix," said Agent Quinn. "Better call this in, pronto."

"First, we shake out the other loser," said Agent Mathison.

They walked out. I felt like a puddle of fat.

THIRTY-ONE

Tough guy peed his pants," said Agent Mathison.

"Understandable, the jam he's in," said Agent Quinn.

"Your fat friend tells us Tom is working with the aliens," said Agent Mathison. "You can confirm that and maybe save your pathetic yellow-stained self, or you can continue to play tough and suffer the consequences."

What consequences, I thought. *I'm thirteen years old. What can they do to me?*

"Don't think," said Agent Quinn in his phony sympathetic voice, "that being a kid protects you from consequences. In war, kids suffer worse than grownups. And we consider this a war. You're not going to walk away."

"Oh, he'll walk, all right," said Agent Mathison. "After we release him in a few months, he'll walk right into a juvenile facility. Those gangbangers love tough guys with zits who pee in their pants."

"So tell us," said Agent Quinn. "Did Alessa tell us the truth? Is Tom in contact with the aliens? Because if she didn't . . ." He looked at Agent Mathison, who gave him her nasty smile.

I took a deep breath—I couldn't help myself. Poor Lessi. She must have figured it didn't matter if she told them. They'd probably figured it out anyway. *Okay, tell them what they already know. No more.*

"It's true."

"Where are they?" said Agent Mathison.

"I don't know," I said.

"When is the last time you saw an alien?"

"If Hercules was an alien, then the last time I saw one was when he showed up at school."

"That's what Alessa said too," said Agent Quinn, smiling at him. "We're going to turn off the lights and music and let you nap for a while."

"But first," said Agent Mathison, "what do aliens look like?"

"Like us," I said.

"Who do you know who were aliens?"

"Dr. Traum, the school psychologist last year. And Hercules, I guess."

"You think Tom could be an alien?" asked Agent Quinn. His question came so casually, I wondered if he didn't remember that I'd already said no.

Carefully, I said, "I guess anyone could be an alien. You. Her."

"Or you," said Agent Quinn.

"Nah," said Agent Mathison. "Aliens don't pee in their pants."

"So," Agent Quinn continued, "you're trying to make us believe that neither Tom nor his twin is an alien?"

"Twin?" That hit me between the eyes. How did they know that?

"One or both?"

"No, no, neither of them is an alien."

"Neither," said Agent Quinn, and he high-fived Agent Mathison. "Twins. Now we got it."

They cackled as they walked out of the room. They left the music and the lights on. I closed my eyes and tried to fall into space. I wanted to go to sleep and not wake up.

THIRTY-TWO

EN ROUTE TO CAPE CANAVERAL, FLA.
2012

O N the helicopter, I tried to get into the Lump's mind, but it was like the inside of a computer, all passageways, compartments, and firewalls. I had expected his mind to be sloppy, like him, but he was so focused on the details of the flight—keeping Ronnie, Buddy, and me in our harnesses, giving directions to the pilots over his headset, and looking around for planes that might be following us—that his mind was a humming grid.

I had a lot of questions but I'd have to wait.

I'd never been in a chopper before and it was noisier and more uncomfortable than I'd imagined. I couldn't believe that Ronnie and Buddy were actually dozing. I watched the land change from farm to beach. I saw signs on rooftops for alligator wrestling. *We're definitely in Florida now,* I thought. Then I saw a huge airfield with giant hangars. I spotted a rocket ship. We landed.

My legs were wobbly for a couple of minutes after we climbed out of the chopper and followed the Lump into a building. A guard tried to stop Ronnie from taking Buddy inside, but the Lump showed him a badge and said something in a sharp voice. My hearing wasn't working yet.

The Lump led us into a cafeteria. He piled a lot of food onto his tray and gestured for us to do the same. I didn't have much of an appetite. Neither did Ronnie, but he got food that Buddy would eat. We all got lots of water.

We were sitting at a table when a tall woman whose shoes made a clacking sound marched up to us. Three guys in dark suits who looked like Agent Brown were behind her.

The Lump wiped his beard and jumped up. "Director. This is Tom and Ronnie."

She squatted down to pat Buddy. "And who are you, you adorable cocker spaniel, you?" The dirty little dog licked her hand. I could see she liked that.

"That's Buddy," said Ronnie.

"What a sweetheart," said the director. But she was looking at Ronnie, studying him hard.

Finally, she stood up. "And the famous Tom." She gave me a once-over. "On TV, you look more muscular."

She scared me. She seemed really tough. And smart. I tried a mind probe but hit cement.

"Good work, Agent Novak," she said to the Lump. "The other two kids are on their way. We're planning liftoff at zero dark thirty."

"We'll be ready," said the Lump.

She gave Ronnie and me another round of once-overs, then broke off a piece of the Lump's hamburger and bent over to feed it to Buddy. The little traitor *smiled* at her. She bent over farther and kissed the top of his head before she clacked off.

Ronnie rolled his eyes at me.

The Lump sat down. "Okay. We'll have a chance to talk before we go."

"Go where? Talk about what?" I said.

The Lump sighed, and food dribbled out of his mouth onto his red whiskers. "Old times? Didn't we have fun when I lived in your house?" he said.

"You kidding? It was a totally crummy experience," I said.

"How's your mom?"

"Stepmom."

"Nice lady. How is she?" He kept smiling as though he wanted to make a friendly connection.

"Who knows? She's traveling for her job all the time."

"Your grandpa takes good care of you."

"What's on your mind, Lump?"

Ronnie gave me a strange look but the Lump just nodded. "Okay, how about this. Todd and Alessa are not critical to this operation. I'm their only hope. You cooperate or they evaporate."

We need to do something now, Dr. Traum. They're in trouble.

The Primary People do not intervene, John. You know that.

I know it's wrong not to take responsibility for what we've done.

As your sons would say: whatever.

I'll make a deal with you.

You're a prisoner, in no position to bargain.

I will promise to give up the rebellion forever if you keep the boys and their friends safe.

I can only promise to send them help now.

That's good enough, Dr. Traum. The twins can do the rest.

THIRTY-THREE

EDDIE
EN ROUTE TO SOMEWHERE IN NORTHERN VIRGINIA
2012

Hop on, Eddie.

I was only a step ahead of the Browns when I spotted Hercules in a black leather jacket and black helmet on a motorcycle growling at the curb. He tossed me a white helmet. I put it on as I leaped onto the back.

We have to stop meeting like this. He laughed like a maniac.

Then we were in traffic. Hercules drove like a maniac.

Good job, Eddie. You're finally getting groovy.

I felt terrific. I forgot I was cold and hungry and had to pee like crazy. We rode over a bridge and out of the city. We rode for a long time, past rows of suburban houses and into farm country. We turned up a two-lane road, then a one-lane dirt road past a farmhouse surrounded by empty fields. I noticed a white van parked outside the farmhouse. Hercules kept going until we came to the woods. He pulled into the trees and stopped. I ran off to pee. When I came back, he was leaning against a tree, his green eyes staring into the distance. I thought I could make out the farmhouse we had seen earlier.

"What are you looking at?"

"Concentrate."

It was like focusing binoculars at Scout camp. After a while, the white farmhouse grew larger in my sight. Clearer. Powers!

"What's going on?"

"We'll wait for dark. When the space shuttle to Riverboat arrives for us."

"Riverboat?"

"That's what Dr. Traum calls our mobile space station. Mark Twain was a riverboat pilot."

"Then what?"

"We'll hitch a ride to Homeplace."

"Dad's there!" I felt excitement like bubbling water inside me.

"He's looking forward to seeing you."

"Will Tom be there?" When Hercules nodded, I asked, "What about Ronnie and the others?"

"You'll have to get those details from Dr. Traum."

"I have a lot of questions."

"He'll answer them. Dr. Traum likes you. He considers you authentic, pure. Sort of like Huckleberry Finn."

"How do you know so much about what Dr. Traum thinks?"

"He and I share a lot of, um, thoughts." Hercules's voice got softer as he spoke, and his body relaxed against the tree. I thought he seemed like a teammate, someone on my side. I was feeling more comfortable talking to him.

"Can you answer some questions?"

He thought for a moment, then sighed and said, "I'll try."

"So these aliens, Primary People—they created the Earths like God did?"

"That's a little heavy, Eddie. Our scientists designed a number of planets around the universe. But we didn't create them from scratch. In every case, one planet already existed and we then constructed a second, a clone, some years younger so we could study different species, see how each evolved."

I had the weird feeling that Hercules was sounding like Dr. Traum.

"In Earth's case, the original—EarthOne, Tom's planet—existed for billions of years before we moved in. Turns out, human beings were the most complicated of the creatures we studied. Made the most trouble for themselves."

"So who made the Primary People?"

"That's what we hoped to find out from these studies. The secrets of the universe. We didn't create human beings, Eddie—we copied them so we could study them. Dr. Traum took particular interest in the United States because it's the most complicated country in the most complicated planet, the one that has the potential to do the most damage and the most good."

"The idea of the tour was to get the good going, right?"

"That's right."

Hercules's smile encouraged me. I thought I might start understanding things. "So is it going to happen? Are we going to save the Earths?"

"Doesn't look too good right now, does it?"

"I don't get it. If the Primary People have all these powers, why don't they save the Earths?"

Hercules sighed again. "When the Primary People began their scientific experiments, the Supreme Council made a law that could not be broken. We would never intervene in the affairs of a planet we were studying."

"You would just stand there and let terrible things happen?"

"I know it sounds cruel, but we had to stay scientists, not gods. We couldn't make even tiny adjustments that would have made life on the Earths better. You ever hear of the butterfly effect?"

"No."

"Some little thing causes bigger things to happen and changes the course of history. A butterfly beats its wings in a certain way and starts a hurricane. You understand?"

I was trying to understand when Hercules cocked his head, nodded, and said, "The Riverboat shuttlecraft is in our atmosphere. It'll be landing soon."

I wanted to ask about the others again, even though Hercules had already told me that I'd have to find out details from Dr. Traum. I hadn't believed Erin when she'd told me everyone had gone home. Apparently I didn't have to ask again—Hercules was inside my mind and answered my unspoken question.

"Tom, Ronnie, and Buddy are with your pal the Lump. Your grandfather is on his own, doing some other work for us. Alessa and Todd are being held by government agents in that farmhouse over there."

"Let's bust them out."

"I thought you'd never ask, Captain Eddie."

THIRTY-FOUR

TOM
CAPE CANAVERAL, FLA.
2012

THE spaceship looked less like a rocket than like two jet airplanes, one riding piggyback on the other. Both had the words FRIENDSHIP ONE painted on their fuselages. They were being fueled from giant trucks marked FRIENDSHIP COMMAND. Dozens of workers in bright blue jumpsuits swarmed over the planes. They all had the word FCOM on their backs.

"What's with the 'Friendship One'?" I asked.

"It means we come in peace," said the Lump.

"Do you?"

"I do. I hope they do, too," said the Lump. The way he said it, I didn't think he believed it either.

"Those things really go into space?" asked Ronnie.

"The big question is," said the Lump, "*do they come back?* They haven't been fully tested yet. Now there's no time."

"So we're the guinea pigs," said Ronnie.

"More like hostages," I said.

"Right," said the Lump. "We figure the aliens won't shoot us down if you're on board."

I imagined Ronnie thinking, *You figure wrong, Lump. Dr. Traum is as big a snake as you are.*

I looked at Ronnie. Something in his eyes told me I hadn't imagined that.

I felt nervous. How much did the Lump know? I still couldn't get into his head. I wondered where Eddie was. I hadn't dared try to make contact with him while the Lump was nearby. The Lump had an equipment bag hanging from his shoulder with a wire going up into his ear. If he could monitor space chatter between Homeplace and the Earths, he might be able to pick up transmissions between Eddie and me.

Just thinking about Eddie started me vibrating, from my toes right up to my scalp. It felt as though Eddie was inside a washing machine. Or maybe on a motorcycle.

"Saddle up," said the director. She was wearing a blue FCOM jumpsuit too.

"Aren't we waiting for a couple more?" said the Lump. He looked puzzled and I thought his mind might be open for a second or two. I probed in fast. I got pictures of Britzky and Alessa.

"Can't wait," said the director. She looked grim. When the Lump shot her a questioning look, she gave him one of those not-now head shakes.

I stabbed into her mind. I imagined *No word from Mathison and Quinn.* What did that mean?

We followed the director and the Lump up a long metal ladder into the piggyback plane. Inside, it looked less like a regular plane than like a smaller version of the bridge of the Starship *Enterprise* from *Star Trek*. People in blue jumpsuits were sitting at banks of dials and levers under walls of screens. In the middle of the main bridge were five big swivel chairs. Two men and a woman were already seated. The director and the Lump took the end chairs.

Armed guards led Ronnie, Buddy, and me to seats in the back of the bridge.

The guy in the middle seat—the pilot, I figured—leaned over toward the director and said, "Good to go."

"How long's the trip?" she asked.

"We're only going up to the edge of space, the Karman line, about sixty-two miles above Earth's surface," said the pilot.

"That's where the aliens have been transmitting and receiving from," said the Lump.

"They better be there," said the director. "Or Agent Novak walks home."

The pilot and the crew laughed, but the Lump shrugged and said, "Something's there. It could be a planet, a space platform, maybe a guy in an inner tube floating along with a solar cell phone."

Even I laughed. It was the only funny thing I'd ever heard the Lump say. But his face was serious. The director wasn't laughing. She gave me the chills.

THIRTY-FIVE

AGENT Mathison shoved me into the van, harder than she had to. I bumped my knee. I could feel skin scrape off.

Britzky was curled up in the back of the van, his knees up to his chest, his head jammed between his knees. His arms were folded over his head. He was a Britzky blob. Every so often, the blob shook, as if he was crying.

"Have fun, kids," said Agent Mathison. She slammed the back door and climbed behind the wheel. She was yelling at Agent Quinn to hurry up so they could phone in the news about the twins.

I lost it. I started crying too. I had never felt so sad and low and helpless. I had betrayed my friends, the only people who could help us.

Agent Quinn climbed into the passenger seat, complaining about his cell phone. No reception. Agent Mathison gunned the van and peeled out. I fell

backwards and banged my head against the van's back
door.

I smelled a bathroom kind of stink. Urine. I noticed
a dark, damp-looking stain on Britzky's pants. Ewww.
Then I felt bad, realizing how terrible he must have felt.
Poor Britzky, the tough guy. They must have really
worked him over.

*Woman up, Lessi! Got to be strong. He's going to need your
help. You're going to need his help.*

Britzky stirred. His head came up. He looked awful
—eyes red, skin gray, forehead zits like an LED board.
He mumbled something.

I scooted on my butt over to him on the ridged cold
metal floor. I timed my scoots to the rocking of the
speeding van.

"I told them," blubbered Britzky.

"What?" I said. But I knew. I was glad it wasn't
only me.

"Twins. Couldn't help it."

"Me too."

Now we were both crying. Britzky's head went back
down between his knees.

I cried myself out. Then I took a deep breath and
reached out to Britzky. The urine smell hit me. I didn't
want to hug him, so I put my hands on his knees. Had to
buck him up.

"I need you, Todd," I said.

Slowly, his head came up again. I could almost see Britzky struggling to pull himself together. His shoulders straightened. He wiped his runny nose on the sleeve of his Tech Off! hoodie. He was a total mess. Like me.

He beckoned me closer. I tried to close my nostrils without touching them, then thought, *Get past it, Lessi.*

He whispered into my ear, "You say anything about them being half aliens?" When I shook my head, he said, "Me neither. That's something."

The van was racing and Agent Quinn was shouting curses. "Still no cell reception."

Agent Mathison said, "We'll be out of the boonies in a few minutes."

"Hey. There's also no power in my cell."

Agent Mathison made a noise through her nose. "I told you to make sure it was charged."

"I did."

"Here." Through the cage I saw her hand him her phone.

Agent Quinn said, "No juice in yours, either."

Agent Mathison cursed. "I'll stop in a minute. I've got a charger in my bag."

"Don't you think we better call in the twin intel ASAP?"

"Yeah, but I want to lose these jerks on my tail. There's a gas station a mile up."

The van slowed. I got my head up in time to see a motorcycle whip past us. There were two guys on the bike and there was something familiar about them.

My heart actually leaped, like in the vampire novels I used to read.

I hugged Britzky. "It's going to be all right."

We pulled into a gas station. I noticed a motorcycle leaning up against the building, hidden behind some bushes. A short, skinny guy in a black leather jacket, wearing a black bandanna on his head and aviator glasses, walked to the van.

"Look at this punk," said Agent Mathison.

"Who do you expect pumps gas out here?" said Agent Quinn.

"At least you get your windows cleaned," said Agent Mathison. She jerked her thumb toward the back.

I turned around. The guy wiping the back window and grinning at us was Eddie.

THIRTY-SIX

'D never been on a plane—much less a spaceship—
before. The takeoff was noisy and bumpy. I squeezed
Buddy until he started squirming. *Sorry.* I felt breakfast coming up into my throat. It tasted worse this time.
I swallowed it back down. That tasted even worse. My
mouth was dry. I was scared. Tom must have noticed,
because he smiled at me and gave me a little tap on the
shoulder. That surprised me. He was trying to make me
feel better. It did make me feel better until I thought,
Things must really be bad for Tom to act nice.

Friendship One climbed for a while. The people in
blue jumpsuits were busy with levers and dials. On the
screens in front of them I could see views from all around
us, Earth getting smaller and the sun getting dimmer and
the moon paler and space darker.

No escape now. For the first time since I'd been on
my own, there was literally no way out. *I'm in a spaceship*

heading to wherever, I thought, *and I can't just slip away and get back on the road. Trapped. And who knows what's up there?* Even when those G-men had had me, I had been thinking about how to escape, imagining that Eddie would come for me. Never thought it would be Tom.

I looked at Tom now. He was staring at the back of the pilot's head as if he was trying to get into his mind. Sometimes I thought he could do that. I was always careful to jumble up my thoughts when he was staring at me. Sometimes I thought I could feel a little tickle in my brain, as if Tom was poking at it. Now I hoped he was getting into the pilot's mind, maybe finding out what was going on. Maybe even learning how to fly this plane.

Sooner or later, someone was going to find out the truth about me, and it would be too bad if it was someone like Keith or Dr. Traum who found out first, before my friends did. Eddie deserved to be the first to know, but I wasn't sure how he would take it after all this time. He was a straight arrow. Maybe he'd feel I'd lied to him. He might be angry and hurt.

Then there was Alessa. She was a good, kindhearted person. She might help me. Britzky wouldn't care—he might even say he'd known all along. I wondered about Tom. He wasn't as mean as I had always thought.

A voice over a loudspeaker said, "PREPARE TO LAUNCH."

"Ready for launch," said the pilot.

Keith looked around, making sure we were all strapped in. He didn't want us to get hurt. He needed us.

WHOP.

It felt as if we'd been shot out of a cannon. We all jerked back into our seats. On the screens, the big plane was falling away and the piggyback plane with us inside was flying farther into space. Earth got even smaller behind us and space up ahead got darker and deeper.

My ears popped.

"Don't worry about that," said the pilot. "The pressure adjusts automatically."

The popping stopped, but it felt as though there were cotton in my ears. It took a moment before I realized Tom was talking to me.

"You okay?" He sounded as if he cared. Or maybe he was like Keith—he needed me for something.

"Yeah."

"What do you think happened to Alessa and Britzky?"

I shrugged. "You worried about them?"

"Duh." He looked at me in a funny way. I felt that mind tickle.

"Cut that out," I said.

"Cut what out?"

"Trying to get in my head."

"How can you tell?"

"There's like a little tickle."

He frowned. "Got to work on that."

Tom touched my arm and pointed at Keith, who was leaning across the pilot and the other men to say to the director, "Do you want to review your proposals to the aliens?"

She shook her head. "This is not a negotiation, Agent Novak. I'm giving them an ultimatum. They can allow us to use their planet as a space station or we can blast them out of the sky."

"Perhaps we might start from a friendlier position, Director," said Keith. "All the years I've been monitoring them, I've never picked up any hostile vibrations."

"Exactly," she said. "If these aliens were any kind of real threat, they would have invaded Earth and taken us over years ago. So we have nothing to worry about."

Keith sighed and leaned back in his chair. He looked unhappy.

I could see that Tom was fighting to keep his mouth shut. He lost. He shouted out, "What if they're trying to make the universe a better place?"

The director said over her shoulder, "Tom, you're too old to believe in Santa Claus and the Easter Bunny. The aliens are only out for themselves."

"We're not like you," Tom said. "We're not even human beings."

I could tell Tom knew he'd made a mistake even before the director and Keith whirled around in their seats to face him.

"What do you mean by 'we,' Tom?" the director asked.

THIRTY-SEVEN

FELT hot and cold, standing in the front of the shuttle as it headed toward Riverboat. All I could think about was seeing Dad again. For two years, I had thought he was dead, and then, six months ago, I saw him for just a moment as Dr. Traum's prisoner. Dad had let himself be captured so Tom and I could go free. I had cried as I'd watched him go up an open elevator into the belly of Riverboat.

Before the bay doors had closed behind him that day, I had yelled, "Dad!" and I thought he'd looked at me and smiled. I thought I heard him transmit, *See you later, alligator!* That was one of our favorite expressions.

I was thinking of that when Alessa and Britzky squeezed my arms. They could tell that Dad was on my mind. They were excited for me. I felt really good about them as my friends.

Rescuing them had been so groovy.

I don't know how Hercules had locked the front doors of the van from the outside, but the agents were inside, banging on the doors, while I melted the back door lock to let Alessa and Britzky out. I had been psyched until I'd realized that had been strictly newbie-boobie stuff for a halfie. I needed to do better with my powers.

After Alessa hugged me, Britzky had started to hug me, then stopped as if he had remembered something. He backed away, and I saw the stain on his pants.

"Forget it," I said. "I did that once in a football game."

It wasn't true, but it was worth lying for the way he said, "Thanks."

The guy who ran the gas station had been busy in the back when we pulled in, and now he came out running and yelling. He had a shotgun in his hands.

I looked at Hercules, who grinned at me. His arms were folded across his chest. "You know how to deal with this."

It was almost too easy. The moment the gun started wiggling in the gas guy's hand, I had an excellent idea. I imagined the snake taking the bottom of the guy's pants in his fangs and trying to pull them off. The guy frantically unbuckled his belt, dropped his pants, and jumped out of them. Then he turned and ran away.

I imagined the snake slithering after him, and then I picked up the pants and handed them to Britzky.

Hercules clapped his hands. "You're not as dumb as you look, Eddie."

Britzky went into the bathroom to change while Alessa went inside the station and found the food and soda machines. She didn't have any money, so I cracked them open for her—more newbie-boobie stuff, no imagination. I felt bad about stealing, but when I heard the two agents yelling and banging inside the locked van, I thought, *Well, under the circumstances . . .*

We were filling a bag with cookies and water when a gray box with wings about the size of the van landed in a field behind the gas station. I thought, *That has to be the shuttlecraft.*

We had piled in, all four of us. The shuttle had lifted straight up. And now, minutes later, Earth was the size of a basketball below us.

"That was amazing, Eddie," said Britzky. "What made the guy drop the gun and take off his pants?"

"The snake made him do it," I said.

"You made him think there was a snake?" said Alessa. "Just with your mind?"

"Your alien powers," said Britzky. "Could you get into my mind?"

"I haven't tried," I said. That was true.

"Better not," said Alessa.

"You're my friends," I said. "Why would I need to?"

Alessa and Britzky looked at each other. What did that look mean? I thought about trying to get into their minds to find out but decided it would be wrong.

"Heads up," said Hercules, pointing to the shuttle's rearview screens. "We've got company."

A blue craft shaped like an airliner, the words FRIENDSHIP ONE on its fuselage, was cruising behind us.

"They're less than a half hour away," said Hercules. "Maybe you can tune Tom in. Space is pretty clear here."

I felt dumb for not coming up with that idea myself. I focused all my energy into piercing the plane's blue skin. I picked up a fuzzy image of Buddy right away, then Ronnie and Tom.

Yo, bro.

Where are you, Eddie?

In front of you. Heading to Riverboat. Alessa and Britzky are here.

They're okay?

Yeah.

Is Dad on Riverboat?

I hope so, Tom.

So's that creep Dr. Traum.

Hercules chuckled and I said, "Tom didn't really mean that."

"Of course he did," said Hercules, his voice sounding even more like Dr. Traum's. "You never have to apologize for honesty among Primary People. And as Mark Twain said, 'If you tell the truth, you don't have to remember anything.'"

Eddie, you still there?

Yeah.

I've got to make this quick. We can't trust Lump and the director. Lump might be able to hear our conversations. And there are soldiers on board here and they have guns.

I heard static, then nothing. I looked at Hercules.

"Tom's in trouble."

"Tom can take care of himself," said Hercules. "Like you."

The shuttle bumped against something and Hercules disappeared. His voice was inside my head. *We're here. Your dad's waiting for you.*

THIRTY-EIGHT

F it were my movie, the scene of Eddie and his dad running toward each other would have been in slow motion. Alessa and I had been right behind Eddie as he'd walked through the passageway connecting the shuttlecraft to Riverboat. We had followed him into a docking area with room for other spaceships and then through a long hallway that led to a brightly lit white auditorium.

Dr. Traum had been standing on the front of the auditorium stage. He was the same short, skinny guy I remembered from six months ago, with a pale, smooth ordinary face, easy to forget except for the glittering green eyes. He was dressed in a white shirt that came down to his knees and black pants.

Behind him were maybe fifty people—really more like shapes—sitting in rows on the stage. They were grouped together by the colors of their long shirts—

purple, red, and green. They looked sort of human, but their faces all looked alike, even with different skin colors and hair lengths.

Watching the shapes and colors on stage shift and meld and separate, I felt as if I were in a dream. I remembered when I'd mentioned the Mark Twain book *A Connecticut Yankee in King Arthur's Court* back in the cafeteria when Hercules had first showed up. I hadn't said that the whole story in the book turned out to be a dream for the hero after he was knocked out cold by a guy nicknamed Hercules. Did I want all of this to be just a dream?

Alessa had grabbed my arm then. "Look!"

A tall, thin man in a long white shirt like Dr. Traum's had jumped off the stage and started running toward us.

Eddie had started running toward him.

They slammed into each other's arms. They hugged for a long time. I think they were both crying.

"This is so sweet," said Alessa now. We both giggled. We were feeling a lot better after all the water and cookies. I was even happy in my greasy gas-station pants, compared to what I'd been wearing. They almost fit around the waist. The legs were rolled up.

We were close enough to hear any conversation between Eddie and his dad, but they weren't saying anything. After a while, they pulled apart just enough to look at each other. Then they touched foreheads. I figured they were doing their telepathy thing, mind to mind.

It seemed like a long time before they totally unhugged, but they kept their arms linked. Eddie pulled his dad toward us. "These are my best friends, Alessa and Britzky. They were with us at the insane asylum last year. This is my dad, John Tudor."

"You've been very good friends to Eddie and Tom. Welcome." He had a nice deep voice. He gave each of us a hug. "You've been in danger and you've been brave."

"Not so brave," I said. I looked at Alessa, who nodded me on. "We need to tell you something. The agents back on EarthOne know that Tom and Eddie are twins. We told them. We didn't mean to—we were hungry and tired, and it just came out. I'm sorry."

"I'm surprised you held out as long as you did," Mr. Tudor said. "That was strong and brave. Don't worry. By the time the agents communicate with their superiors, it won't matter."

"What's happening here, Mr. Tudor?" said Alessa.

"The Supreme Council of the Primary People"— he gestured at the shapes on the stage—"have assembled. They represent the three governing bodies on Homeplace. The ones in green are Science; the ones in purple are Politics; the red ones are Art. They are going to make a decision on when to destroy the Earths."

Before I could ask a question, I heard the loud scraping of metal on metal below us. It had to be another spaceship docking in Riverboat's bay.

Mr. Tudor pulled Eddie toward a side door, opened it, and pushed Eddie into another room. "Stay out of sight."

Alessa pulled my sleeve. "Did he say they're deciding on *when* to destroy the Earths? Not *whether*?"

"Decisions can be changed," I said. "The twins can do it."

I hoped I sounded more sure than I felt.

THIRTY-NINE

I PROBED the director's mind. All I found were sharp edges and red flags. I could tell she didn't like me even before she whispered to the Lump, "I don't like him."

"When this is over, Director," said the Lump in a soothing voice, "you can toss him into space. Right now, we need him alive. He may turn out to be a bargaining chip."

The Lump winked at me. I couldn't tell if he was signaling that he was on my side or on her side or if he was just telling me to keep my mouth shut. His mind was in lockdown.

"Get that brat out of here," said the director.

Two guards were lifting me out of my chair when the pilot said, "Destination in view."

I spotted what had to be Riverboat in a corner of one of the flight-deck screens.

"That's it?" said the director. She sounded disappointed.

"What were you expecting?" I said. "The Death Star?"

"Kind of," she said. "What was the place where the Borg hung out?"

"The Unicomplex," I said.

"You would know that," said the director.

"I think that's just a floating space station," said the Lump, indicating the picture on the screen in front of them. "It's not their planet."

"Homestead?" said the director.

"Homeplace," I snarled. "Better get it right if you expect them to listen to you."

She shook her head. "I will deal with you later." She signaled the guards. They dropped me back into the chair. One of them gave my arm a little twist on the way down. I couldn't resist imagining one of his fingers breaking. He let out a cry of pain and clutched his hand. It was all in his head and his finger was physically fine. I shouldn't have done it, though, as good as payback feels for the moment. Luckily, no one else was paying much attention. If people saw stuff like that happen, they could figure out that I have powers. I had to watch myself.

Riverboat slowly filled the screen. Its belly was open and lights shone from inside. After a while, a tube slid out and attached itself to our ship, right over the main hatch.

The hatch popped open. A digitized voice said, "You may enter. The passageway is pressurized for your safety."

"Think we can trust them?" said the director.

"If they wanted to blow us away," said the Lump, "we'd be dust by now."

Buddy started barking at the screen. Ronnie shot me a smile. I imagined I heard him think, *Buddy knows Eddie's there.*

"Let's go," said the director. She waved two armed guards to lead the way and two to bring up the rear.

The tube connecting us to Riverboat swayed as we walked over its shifting plastic plates. Buddy scampered ahead, squealing between barks, scurrying out of the tube and over a metal floor into a brightly lit white auditorium.

Buddy ran to a closed door, went up on his back legs, and began scratching. I figured Eddie was behind the door, hiding so that the director and the Lump wouldn't know there were two of us.

Ronnie grabbed my arm. "Look!"

Alessa and Britzky were waving at us.

Next to them was Dad.

I paused for an instant in the doorway of the auditorium. I guess I felt a little shy. But then Dad opened his arms and I raced into them.

FORTY

BRITZKY nudged me with an elbow and pointed at a tall woman storming into the auditorium at the head of a pack of tough-looking people with guns.

"Who's in charge here?" she shouted.

Tom and his dad unhugged and Dr. Traum said, "They are in charge," pointing to the colored shapes on the stage. "The Supreme Council of the Primary People."

The woman said, "I am the director of the National Security Agency's Bureau of Unidentified Flying Objects and Extraterrestrial Life Forms." She waited for all that to sink in. Then she said, "And I am a special envoy from the president of the United States."

"You are welcome," said Dr. Traum. "But first, no weapons are permitted here. Please put down your guns."

"That's not going to happen," said the director.

"I must insist," said Dr. Traum.

"Insisting would be a mistake," said the director.

It was a tense moment.

Dr. Traum looked at Tom, who looked at his dad, who nodded.

Tom swept his eyes across the guards. They began screaming and throwing their guns away as if they had turned into . . . snakes!

Britzky and I grinned at each other. I said, "Great twin minds with a single thought."

"Snakes are getting old," said Britzky. "Hope they have some other ideas."

Tom looked at us. I could almost feel him asking us to get the guns out of the room before the guards figured out the snakes were only in their imagination. Britzky must have gotten the same message, because we both hurried over, scooped up the guns, and dumped them outside the auditorium.

When we got back, Tom and his dad gave us the thumbs-up. Dr. Traum was gesturing at the director. "Please, be seated."

She didn't look so sure of herself now. She turned and I spotted the Lump right behind her. They looked at each other, then the woman nodded, and they took seats in the front row. So the Lump *was* working for the government. We had figured that.

"There's Ronnie," whispered Britzky.

Ronnie was in the back of the auditorium, looking small and scared. I waved to him. He hurried over, looking grateful. I gave him a hug. I was surprised how easily Ronnie let me do it. He'd always seemed like a guy who hated to be hugged. He shook hands with Britzky. They *almost* hugged. When we sat down, Buddy jumped into Ronnie's lap and licked my hand, then Britzky's. What a family!

Dr. Traum raised his hands. "The Supreme Council of the Primary People has assembled to make its final decision on the termination of the Earths."

The director looked confused. "Earths?"

Dr. Traum said, "There are two planet Earths. The Primary People created a second Earth, a half century younger than the first, as an experiment."

"That's nonsense," said the director. "It took billions of years for Earth to evolve."

"That's true," said Dr. Traum. "And it took us only one hundred years to clone it."

"These . . . *creatures* are insane," said the director to the Lump, who looked as if he was trying to hush her up. She glared at him.

The stage began to vibrate as the shapes on the grandstand shimmered, melted into one another, then slowly shook back to their original colors and shapes.

Dr. Traum said, "The Council wants to know: Why are you here?"

"It is our intention," said the director, "to form an interplanetary alliance between Homeplace and Earth. Or the Earths, if you will."

Dr. Traum gave her his cold smile. "What can you offer us besides extreme weather, unstable governments, and the possibility of nuclear explosions?"

"Goodwill and peace,'" the director said.

The grandstand erupted in laughter.

"The Council finds that ridiculous," said Dr. Traum. "There has rarely been peace on your warlike planets."

"Peace between my planet and yours," said the director. "Otherwise, we would have to regard you as hostile and we would be prepared to blast Homeplace out of the sky."

"That unfriendly attitude is exactly why the Council is considering when to destroy the Earths," said Dr. Traum. "For the good of the universe."

The laughter got nastier as the colors and shapes on the grandstand merged into a Crayola pudding.

Britzky was shivering.

"Are you okay?" I whispered.

"I'm great," he whispered back. "This is like being inside history, like standing there while the Founding Fathers wrote the U.S. Constitution."

"Except this could get us dead," I said.

"Those were pretty dangerous times, too," said Britzky.

The director said, "Let me be completely honest. It's no secret that Earth is in trouble. Extreme weather will eventually make our planet unable to sustain life. Therefore, the American people would like to enter into a relationship with the Primary People. We hope we might be able to share your planet when we are no longer able to live on ours."

"Let me ask you again," said Dr. Traum. "What can you possibly offer us?"

"We can offer you continued existence," said the director. "You can accept our offer or suffer the consequences."

"Threats," said Dr. Traum, "from the bully of the universe."

The grandstand on stage went berserko. There was screaming and barking as the colors spun like a kaleidoscope.

"I figured it out," whispered Britzky. "They're holograms. The real Primary People must be somewhere else. Maybe on Homeplace."

"How do you know stuff like that?" I was impressed.

"Like I told you, everything's online," he said. "If you know where to look."

Dr. Traum said, "As you can see, the Council is not amused. It will adjourn now to decide how soon to destroy the Earths."

FORTY-ONE

DAD had pushed me into a library! Four walls covered with books, floor to ceiling. Why couldn't it have been a gym? If I had to wait all by myself, I'd rather be shooting hoops. It's not that I hate books. A book just doesn't fit into my hands the way a ball does. No secret—I'm not a great reader. I have trouble keeping my mind on the words.

There was a table and chair in the middle of the room. There was an open book on the table. *The Adventures of Tom Sawyer* by Mark Twain.

I walked around the room. Maybe I could find a sports book. No luck. There were history books and famous novels I had heard of in school, such as *Uncle Tom's Cabin* and *The Grapes of Wrath,* and lots of books in different languages. There were shelves and shelves of books by Twain.

I went back to the table and looked at *Tom Sawyer.*

Chapter One

"TOM!"

No answer.

"TOM!"

No answer.

*"What's gone with that boy, I wonder?
You TOM!"*

*The old lady pulled her spectacles down and
looked over them about the room; then she put them
up and looked out under them. She seldom or never
looked THROUGH them for so small a thing as a
boy; they were her state pair, the pride of her heart,
and were built for "style," not service—she could
have seen through a pair of stove-lids just as well.*

*She looked perplexed for a moment, and then
said, not fiercely, but still loud enough for the furni-
ture to hear:*

"Well, I lay if I get hold of you I'll—"

It wasn't that bad, I guess, sort of old-timey and slow.
But I didn't feel like reading right then.

I put the book down and put my ear against the door.
I could hear some yelling out there, but I couldn't make
it out. I tried to tune in Tom but got no answer. Just like
the old lady in the book.

I returned to the pages. There was something tucked

into the back. A comic book! A Classics Illustrated version of *Tom Sawyer*.

When I picked it up, a piece of paper fluttered out. It was a letter. To me! From Dad!

Dear Eddie,

I know you'll read this and that's a beginning.

I know you've never thought of yourself as much of a reader, and that could be my fault. We loved playing ball together so much, we didn't spend enough time reading together. I hope we get a chance to work on that. Meanwhile, I think two good books for you to read are The Adventures of Tom Sawyer and The Adventures of Huckleberry Finn. I know you've read the first page of Tom Sawyer, and I bet you thought to yourself that it wasn't so bad but kind of old-fashioned and slow, and you put it down. I'd like you to try it again. But first, let me tell you a little about the story to get you started.

Tom Sawyer is a goodhearted boy who likes to act bad. He's pretty tricky. One time he has to whitewash a fence and he persuades the kids in town to do it — and they pay him to do it, too! He gets to go to his own funeral. He solves a murder, finds buried treasure, and has all kinds of dangerous adventures.

Maybe Tom Sawyer reminds you of your brother, Tom. You'll enjoy the book. And the best part is that there's a second book — even better, I think — about Tom's best pal, a brave kid named Huckleberry Finn, who reminds me of you!

Hope you enjoy your reading. We'll do some together soon.

Love,
Dad

I read the letter twice. I'd never gotten a letter from Dad before. He used to call home every night when he was on the road coaching basketball and tell me about where he was and what he was doing. But he'd never written. The letter made me feel close to him. He did care about us. Dad and I had barely talked when we'd hugged a little while ago. He told me how proud he was of me and we just held on.

I liked the idea that we'd be doing some reading together soon. I decided to read both books, even if it was going to be hard. I knew I could do it. I had been a lousy foul-shooter until I'd started practicing seriously every single day. I started on the comic-book version of *Tom Sawyer* first, figuring it would help me with the real version. When I neared the end, I realized I was actually enjoying reading for the first time in my life.

Bang! The door burst open and Tom ran in. Dad was right behind him.

Group hug.

It was Dad who pushed us apart. "Not much time. The Council is about to come back with a date on which to destroy the Earths. We have one chance to persuade them not to, and it'll take you boys making a speech."

"To say what?" said Tom.

"That's up to you," said Dad. "You need to convince them to spare the Earths, or at least give earthlings more time to make their planets better."

"Both of us?" I asked, hoping it would be Tom.

"Only one of you can go out," said Dad. "We don't want the human beings to know there are two of you. But you can work together, transmitting."

"Let Tom go out," I said. "He's smarter."

"Let Eddie go," said Tom. "Dr. Traum likes him better."

"Dr. Traum likes you both," said Dad. "But I think Eddie should go out. He's had a lot of public-speaking experience lately. Tom can stay here and come up with good ideas. Nothing beats twins working together. Twin powers."

FORTY-TWO

I T took a lot of energy to imagine a peephole in the library door. But not as much as it had taken me a few days ago to bore through a trailer wall to see a fat guy reading a fishing magazine on the toilet.

My powers were improving!

Eddie was standing in front of the auditorium, looking up at the stage. We had swapped clothes, fast, so the director and the Lump wouldn't catch on. Dr. Traum stood in front of a closed curtain, looking down at Eddie. It looked like a staring contest, but I figured they were transmitting. I tuned in.

The Council is angry, Eddie. You'll have one chance to convince them to postpone the Earths' death sentence.

I'm ready, Dr. Traum.

Good old Give-Me-the-Ball Eddie. But I could tell he wasn't all that sure of himself. His jaw was tight so his teeth wouldn't chatter, and his legs were locked so his knees wouldn't quiver. Not like hoops, huh?

What's wrong with you, Tom? Think Dad should have sent you out instead? You suggested Eddie. Get on the team. Give him a pat.

You can do it, big guy, I transmitted to Eddie.

Thanks, bro.

He needed that. It felt good to be his coach, especially for something important, not sports.

Dad was standing in a corner, smiling and nodding. He was hearing us. In the seats behind Eddie were Alessa, Britzky, Ronnie, that dog, and that bigger dirty dog, the Lump, next to the director of that NSA bureau. I was trying to probe their minds when the curtain rose.

The Council was on the grandstand again, green and red and purple pulsing and buzzing. They were holograms, I figured. The real Primary People must have been up on Homeplace.

Dr. Traum said, "Before you announce your decision, members of the Council, I have an appeal. Tom Canty requests an opportunity to speak to you."

The colors on the grandstand shifted and melted together. "We have made our decision!"

I sent Eddie some strong, positive vibrations. **Come out swinging!**

"Wait a minute!" shouted Eddie. "You've got to hear me out."

You could see the grandstand rattle. The Council was not used to being ordered around. There was a loud "Why?"

"Because you don't have any right to just create something and then walk away from it."

The Council didn't like that. The colors mixed and got darker. The buzzing grew louder.

Hit 'em again, Eddie. Tell 'em they have to take responsibility.

"You guys have to take responsibility for your actions. You're putting all the blame on human beings when you should take some yourself."

That struck home. The buzzing faded away. "Speak!"

"I grew up on what you call EarthTwo, but for us it was the only Earth. It's 1958 there now, and we're just starting to think about the problems that EarthOne is dealing with in 2012."

Even Dr. Traum was nodding Eddie on. Whose side was that guy on?

"I don't think you really helped us enough," said Eddie. "You take credit for EarthTwo, okay, but was it just an experiment for you? How can you do all the stuff you did and then not make sure it works out for people?

"Dad taught me that I have to be accountable for

everything I do. He must have learned that from you guys, his people, the Primary People."

Way to go, bro.

It was quiet in the auditorium except for Eddie's breathing. It takes a lot of energy to make a speech like that.

The grandstand sounded meek. "What do you want us to do?"

What do we want them to do, Tom?

It's their problem, Eddie.

"I don't know—I'm not smart enough," said Eddie. "But my dad is. And you guys have to be pretty smart, with all you've done. I know you can figure out how to deal with extreme weather and nukes."

SNAP.

The figures on the stage vanished, sucked into a single spot of light that blinked and went dark like a TV set shutting down.

Dr. Traum stood alone on the stage. "The Council has reconvened to reconsider its vote. Well done, young man."

You're a monster, Eddie—you did great.

We did great, Tommy. Thanks for the coaching.

What a humble guy. I was so proud of him. I felt bad for feeling jealous. And for thinking that he'd need me to supply all his words.

Dad, Alessa, Britzky, and Ronnie surrounded Eddie, grabbing and hugging him. The dog kept trying to jump up on him. I wished I could be with them. But not as long as the Lump, the director, and the *Friendship One* crew were out there.

They were all standing around the Lump, who was staring at a screen in his hand. I imagined a surveillance camera over his shoulder to get a peek at it.

Uh-oh.

What looked like black spaceships were heading toward us.

Suddenly I knew what I needed to do and who I needed to help me.

FORTY-THREE

BUDDY went bananas when the twins changed places again. Eddie went back into the library and a few minutes later Tom came out wearing Eddie's clothes, which were a little loose on him. I wondered if anyone besides me could tell. Buddy was growling and squirming. I had to hold him tight. The director and the Lump didn't seem to notice the switch. They were too busy huddled in a corner, looking at a little screen. Something was up. I had a bad feeling.

Dr. Traum said, "Ladies and gentlemen, the Council will be occupied for a while. There is food in the adjoining room." He waved his arm toward a door in the back of the auditorium. Britzky and Alessa took off toward it.

Tom tapped my arm and jerked his head toward the door that led to the docking bay. When I followed him, Buddy squirted out of my arms and ran to the library door, scratching at it.

"He'll be okay," Tom whispered. "Eddie'll come out after we're gone."

"Gone where?"

Tom just walked faster. My bad feeling grew into an icy ball in my stomach, but I kept following Tom. He had saved me. I trusted him.

Nobody stopped us as we hurried through the tube to *Friendship One*. Once we were on the threshold of the blue spaceship, a guard blocked our way until Tom stared at him. The guard finally stepped aside and smiled at us. When we got to the bridge, the pilot stood up.

"What are you . . . ?"

Tom gave him the stare. "Prepare to, um, split." The pilot got out of our way. Tom grinned at me. "Take over the steering controls."

"Me?"

"Best driver I know." He pointed at one of the big screens. "We don't have much time."

On the screen, six big black rocket ships were heading toward us. No flags, no insignia. Like pirate ships.

"Who are they?"

"What's the opposite of friendship?"

"Where are we going?" I asked.

"We need to lead them away from Riverboat. Back to Earth."

Steering *Friendship One* backwards out of the Riverboat bay was harder than I'd thought. It was a pretty tight fit. Every time the metal of *Friendship One* touched the metal of the Riverboat bay, there was a scraping noise that was worse than a million fingernails dragging over a blackboard.

Tom's eyes were drilling into the pilot's head. I imagined there was a pipeline of thoughts. He could easily do that to me if I had my guard down. I was going to have to talk to him, tell him everything about me, before he found out on his own.

The pilot tapped the microphone. "This is *Friendship One* to security fleet, *Friendship One* to security fleet. Change of orders. Follow us. Repeat: all follow us."

I heard angry squawking but I couldn't understand it. The pilot was yelling into his microphone. Tom was shaking and sweating as he stared at the pilot's head.

There was a bump and I could see on the screens that *Friendship One* was out in space. I gripped the controls and turned the ship around toward Earth.

The fleet was coming right at us.

"What should I do, Tom?"

He couldn't hear me. I figured he was totally focused on keeping control of the pilot's mind. No time for me. But he trusted me. *Best driver I know,* he had said. Tom had said that.

I headed right into them, ready to swerve if any of

the black spaceships came too close. But I figured none of them would want to hit us—this was the director's ship. Even if they thought someone else had taken over, they had to think she was on board. They wouldn't want to smash into her. Or would they? Or would they expect us to swerve away?

It was a big game of chicken.

That was a big deal back on EarthTwo. Two guys would drive at each other. The guy who swerved first was called a coward, a chicken. Stupidest game of all time.

Eddie and I went to a movie once called *Rebel Without a Cause*. A great movie. The hero played chicken against another guy to see who would bail out first before their cars went over a cliff. The hero won because the other guy's sleeve got caught and he couldn't get out of his car before it went over the cliff.

The fleet parted to let us through.

The ice ball in my stomach melted and I felt hot.

Hot and big and strong.

Ronnie rocks!

I wasn't sure what that meant, but the tone in Tom's voice in my head made me feel great. Like the hero in *Rebel*. He was played by James Dean, a great actor.

Earth grew from a dot to a golf ball ahead of us.

I checked the screens. Most of the black ships had

turned and were following us, but one of them had stayed on its course and was heading straight to Riverboat.

The pilot shouted, "Repeat: all ships follow us!"

Through the squawking and static, I heard, "We've got orders to destroy that space station."

Bright red pulsing laser beams shot out of the nose of the black ship and began smashing into Riverboat. I thought I saw pieces of Riverboat break off and drift into space.

Eddie and Buddy were on Riverboat! Alessa and Britzky!

We could go back. Save them.

Keep going. The voice sounded like Dr. Traum's.

I thought, *What about you?*

One of the screens was blazing. Riverboat was on fire.

Keep going. It was Tom's voice this time.

FORTY-FOUR

Just before the first lasers hit, Eddie's dad and Dr. Traum hustled us into the shuttlecraft we had taken to get from the gas station to Riverboat. I was surprised that they got everybody safely aboard, even the director and her soldiers. I would have left them. There were eleven of us crammed together, plus Buddy, who was whimpering in Eddie's arms. I knew how he felt.

We saw Riverboat explode. It wasn't one of those big yellow and red blasts you see on TV shows—it was more like gray chunks breaking apart and floating off into space. The only colors were the red lines firing out of the nose of the black rocket.

Eddie glared at the director and said, "Did you tell them to blow us up?"

She looked down.

"Answer the boy," said the Lump. His voice was cold. So which side was he on? His own, I guessed.

I looked at Alessa. African American faces don't get pale, but they do get that ashy look. She sighed, sounding like an air mattress collapsing. We were in trouble.

"Ah, human beings," said Dr. Traum. "Endlessly interesting, endlessly dangerous."

"Some, but not all," said Eddie's dad.

"Still the idealist, John," said Dr. Traum. "As Mark Twain said, 'Man is the only animal that deals in that atrocity of atrocities, War.'"

The Lump pushed his way closer to the director. "I said, answer the boy."

She took a deep breath. "I had nothing to do with the attack on the space station."

Eddie said, "How would they have known we were all off Riverboat?"

I figured it out. "They thought the director was on *Friendship One* and that she was okay. They didn't care about anyone else. Those were her orders."

The director gave me a killer look. I was right!

Dr. Traum looked at Eddie's dad. "Tell me, John. You still think human beings are worth saving?"

"Of course I do," he said. "Alessa and Todd are worth saving. Ronnie is worth saving. Most people are worth saving and we have no right to choose. She doesn't either." He pointed at the director. "Todd was right. You had this worked out from the start. If the fleet saw *Friendship One* leave, they were supposed to escort you back to Earth and blow up Riverboat."

She made a snorting noise. "We couldn't leave a space platform for some terrorists to take over, could we?"

"Why didn't you tell me?" asked the Lump.

"I don't trust you," she said. "You said you liked the boy." She jerked her head at Eddie. Buddy growled at her.

My head was splitting. These people were even more untrustworthy and dishonest than I had ever imagined. They lied to one another! I could see why the Primary People wanted to get rid of human beings. Well, not all of us.

"We have a more immediate problem," said Dr. Traum. "This shuttle is overloaded. We won't make it to Homeplace unless at least four people are jettisoned."

"The guards can go," said the director.

The four soldiers looked around wildly. It was a good thing they were unarmed.

"Relax." Dr. Traum raised his arms. "We're not overloaded. I just wanted to make my point about the nature of humans: always ready to sacrifice others."

Alessa raised her hand as if she were in class. "Maybe

you need to cop to some of that, Dr. Traum, seeing as how you ran our planets."

"She's right," I said. "Seems like you were ready to sacrifice us for your little experiment. How come you guys never stepped in when you could have made a difference? Like Eddie said, you guys have to take responsibility."

Alessa was smiling at me and I was feeling pretty good until the Lump said, "Who's Eddie? It was Tom who said that when he was talking to the Council."

Dr. Traum smiled. "To be continued. Prepare for landing on Homeplace."

FORTY-FIVE

TOM
SOMEWHERE IN SPACE
2012

TRIED to tune in Eddie. Nothing. Not even static. Not even that deep underwater sound. Were they all gone?

Ronnie had tears in his eyes.

"They could have escaped," I said.

"How?"

"They had that shuttle." I knew I didn't sound very convincing.

"Maybe we're the only ones left," said Ronnie.

The pilot stood up suddenly. "What's going on here?"

I'd lost my concentration and slipped out of his mind. He reached into a mesh case on his belt and pulled out two Sharpie-size rods like the ones I had tried to use in the cafeteria against Hercules so long ago.

"Those are Extreme-Temperature Narrow-Beam Climate Simulators," I said. I put my hands up, pretending to surrender. "Either one can stop a water buffalo."

"You know it," said the pilot. "I want you and your little friend to leave the bridge. *Now.*"

I flicked Ronnie a quick message. ***Keep steering.***

"Please don't shoot," I said as meekly as I could. I stood up and waved my arms to distract him as I sent a probe into his mind. It was hard. He was so intent on getting us off the deck. I kept talking. "The data suggests that the simulators operate on auto-suggestion. That means they aren't really shooting hot or cold. They are causing the target's brain to believe it is being bombarded with an extreme temperature that will disable it."

The pilot smirked. "Maybe you want to find out if that's true."

I wasn't absolutely sure if it was true or not.

I shut down my mind to any suggestion except my own. I imagined steel shutters rolling down with a clang around my brain.

"Move it!" said the pilot. He aimed the rods at me.

"Fire away!"

If I was wrong, I'd be frozen and cooked.

In the moment he fired, his mind opened up. I imagined the beams rattling harmlessly off my steel shutters and bouncing right back into him. He started howling, dropping the little rods and clutching himself. He shivered with cold and collapsed with heat exhaustion.

I was right! It was all in the mind!

My mind.

I remembered back when I'd thought that Tom Canty was only as good as his devices. A week ago? More?

"Tom? You okay?"

I hadn't caught my breath yet, so I just made a fist and threw it up into the air. It was something Eddie would do after scoring a winning basket. But how did I know that? I'd never seen him play basketball. Was part of twin-sense sharing our histories?

The pilot crawled off the bridge. Ronnie and I were alone. The others in the crew had slunk away too. The five black rockets were still following us, but they were getting closer.

The radio crackled. "This is *Security Fleet Two*. Come in, *Friendship One*."

I tried to throw out a probe to the mind of the *Security Fleet Two* pilot, but the distance through space and two ships was too great. Maybe someday I'd be able to do that. If I lived long enough.

Puffs of green and yellow gas burst out of the backs of the black rockets. Superboosters. The spaceships caught up to us, separated, and surrounded us.

"What should I do?" said Ronnie. His little fists were strangling the steering controls.

I was trying to think. As long as they thought the director was on board, they wouldn't open fire on us. They would just herd us back to EarthOne in 2012. Did we want to go there?

Friendship One shuddered and jerked forward, picking up speed. The back of the craft had broken off into a cuplike shape. A parachute bloomed behind it. The cup floated toward EarthOne, which was now as big as a basketball on the screen.

"What was that?" said Ronnie.

"A landing capsule," I said. I'd seen it on TV when astronauts left their spaceships after coming into Earth's atmosphere. "The pilot and the crew just bailed out."

"Is that bad for us?"

"Could be. If the fleet thinks the director is safe, they might open fire on us." I took a breath. "We might not make it, Ronnie."

"What are we going to do?" Ronnie seemed calm. He trusted me.

Before I could tell him that I didn't know, Ronnie stood up and looked into my eyes. His eyes were very blue. I'd never noticed that before. He said, "In case we don't make it, Tom, I've got to tell you something. About myself."

I didn't bother to probe his brain. I knew what he

was going to say. "You don't have to tell me anything, Ronnie. I think you're a good, brave guy, and it doesn't matter to me if you're gay."

I wasn't sure if he'd be glad or angry that I'd figured it out. But I didn't expect him to laugh.

"I always thought you'd be the one to realize the truth, Tom," said Ronnie. "I'm not gay. I'm a girl."

FORTY-SIX

D AD and I were standing close together at the front window of the shuttle and I felt really good. I was finally with my dad again.

But some of that good feeling leaked away as Homeplace grew in the window.

The planet looked awful, like an old apple left out to rot, wrinkled and dry and brown.

"Was it always like this?" I asked.

Dad shook his head. "Once it was as green and wet as the Earths."

The planet filled the front window. The old brown apple had square white spots on it. Poles stuck out of the spots.

"What are those?" I asked.

"The poles are sensors, checking weather and air quality," said Dad. "The square spots are hatches. They lead down into the center of the planet, where we have to live now."

"What happened?" said Britzky.

"Just what we don't want to happen on the Earths," said Dad. "The Primary People are not warlike, so we weren't going to blow ourselves up, but we were pretty stupid and shortsighted when it came to carbon gases and global warming and extreme weather. Now we have a chance to prevent catastrophes on the Earths. How can we not do the right thing?"

Alessa turned to Dr. Traum. "Will you do the right thing?" she asked.

"That's two questions, really," said Dr. Traum. "Can we prevent the catastrophes on Earths, and do we want to?" He tilted his head toward the director, the Lump, and the soldiers whispering in the back of the shuttle. "Human beings don't inspire much confidence."

"They're human beings too," said Dad, pointing to Britzky and Alessa. "Eddie and Tom are half."

"That's true," said Dr. Traum. "Small beacons of hope. Very small."

"Enough for us to do the right thing," said Dad.

Dr. Traum snorted. "We'll see what the Council decides."

A digitized voice said, "Prepare for landing."

The shuttle settled softly on the ground. Clouds of

brown dust covered the windows. We waited for the dust to settle. The nearest white hatch opened. A huge tube snaked up and fastened itself to the side of the shuttle. A door opened. Dr. Traum led us out.

There was an escalator inside the tube that hummed as it took us down to a big elevator. When we were all inside, the elevator whooshed downward. It stopped with a little bump. The elevator door opened onto what looked like a hospital waiting room. People in white coats were walking in and out of smaller rooms with medical equipment.

"Before we can go any farther into Homeplace," said Dr. Traum, "everyone will need to undergo tests and decontamination. We're very concerned about introducing any infectious bacteria or viruses."

The director said, "We are not submitting to any invasive procedures."

"The alternative," said Dr. Traum, "is for you to stay on the surface of Homeplace. I don't think you'd last very long."

We were sent to different examining rooms. At least a dozen people crowded into mine. They sort of looked like human beings except their features were smooth and without much expression. But by the way they were bobbing up and down, I could tell they were excited, really glad to see me. When I concentrated, I felt welcoming vibrations from their minds. I had forgotten for a minute that I'm half Primary People. When I remembered that, they all started bobbing faster. And chattering.

The guy who seemed to be in charge said, "Ahh, Edward Tudor, we have been so looking forward to meeting you." He pumped my hand. He wouldn't let go.

"You know me?" It sounded dumb, especially after they all laughed.

"You are a hero on Homeplace, Edward, as is your brother, Thomas. We've been following your adventures on the Earths for years. You are such a great athlete. And so clever! I particularly liked the way you defeated that gang of baseball thugs by making them think their bats were snakes."

All the white-coated people behind him pretended they were throwing bats away. One of them shouted, "Raiders rule!" They were laughing so hard, they were shaking.

"How did you see that?" I said.

"The monitors have been sending back video of you boys for years." He finally let go of my hand. "I'm Dr. Robinson."

Something clicked in my brain and I said, "A Dr. Robinson was murdered by Injun Joe."

He clapped his hands. "And you're so smart! You've read *The Adventures of Tom Sawyer*."

I didn't want to tell him I'd read only the comic-book version Dad had tucked into the back of the real book.

I changed the subject. "What happens now, Dr. Robinson?"

"Just a quick checkup. You won't feel a thing." He held out a cup attached to a tube. "Breathe in."

As I drifted into dreamland, I saw a blue rocket ship heading toward a sparkling green Earth. But five black rocket ships were attacking it. Ronnie was steering the blue ship and Tom was in the pilot's chair. I sensed they would need my help soon.

FORTY-SEVEN

I FELT a hundred pounds lighter, which seemed goofy for someone who doesn't even weigh a hundred pounds. Just getting those words out—"I'm a girl"—was like turning on the light in a dark basement. It wasn't a secret anymore. I didn't have to feel so scared someone would find out.

And the expression on Tom's face was so cool. He was smiling. He's not mean-looking when he smiles. I was feeling good, remembering him saying, "I think you're a good, brave guy," until I also remembered him saying, "We might not make it."

Big whoop, as Eddie would say. *So now I could be who I really am. Only dead.*

"Maybe not," said Tom.

I had felt the tickle in my brain. "Stop that."

"If you don't want me in your mind, then close it down like you've been doing," said Tom.

"I don't want to be like that anymore," I said. "I want to feel normal."

Tom nodded. "Okay. I won't try to pick your brain anymore."

I wanted to believe that, but Tom's Tom.

I was about to ask him how he felt about my being a girl when the radio crackled again. "This is *Security Fleet Two*. Come in, *Friendship One*."

The black rockets were tightening up around us. "Respond or we'll commence firing."

I said, "What do we do now?"

"We have two choices," said Tom, "neither of them so great. We could give up and let them guide us back to EarthOne, or we could try to break away."

"Where would we go?"

"Back into space? Maybe we could find Homeplace."

"Do we have enough gas? Do you know how to get there?"

Tom shook his head. "I'm sorry." He sounded so sorry I felt bad for him.

"Don't be sorry—you've been great."

"Not great enough. If we go back to EarthOne, we'll be in big trouble."

"What can they do to thirteen-year-old kids?" I said.

"You're thinking 1958 on EarthTwo. It's 2012 on EarthOne, and everybody's cranked up about the war on terror. They put people in jail for years."

"This is *Security Fleet Two*," came from the radio. "We will commence firing in thirty seconds."

"It's me they're after," said Tom. "I can say you're a hostage. You'll be okay." He opened his microphone.

"What are you going to do?"

"Surrender. Follow them in."

"What about EarthTwo?" I said. "There's got to be a way to get there, like maybe a rip in the sky somewhere."

"A rip?

"Yeah. Like the place we slip through. A hole. A door."

The radio again: "Ten seconds before we commence firing."

"Let's find it," said Tom.

I twisted the controls hard and steered *Friendship One* between two of the black rockets. They pulled out of the way.

Tom shut off the microphone. "You're a great driver," he said, laughing. "For a girl."

That *was* pretty funny. I felt relaxed, even though I was focusing hard. The black rockets could be bluffing about shooting us. How could they be so sure the director wasn't on board? Had to take that chance.

I swung left hard, right at a black rocket. It got out of my way.

"More speed," I said.

Tom turned his dials.

All five rockets were behind us now and Earth was growing in the front screen. But which Earth?

"That's EarthOne," said Tom. He must have picked my brain again but I let it go for now.

"How do you know?" It was just a blue-green ball to me.

"I can see the tallest building in the world, the Burj Khalifa."

"The what?"

"It was built about ten years ago. In Dubai."

EarthOne was coming up fast.

"We've got to find that rip, get to EarthTwo," said Tom.

"Federal agents are looking for me and Eddie on EarthTwo. Maybe this isn't so smart," I said.

"Yeah, but EarthTwo in 1958 doesn't have the kind of technology that can track you down in minutes."

Far off to the left, in the darkness of space, I thought I saw a thin gray line.

"Where would we land if we got to EarthTwo?" I asked.

"I don't know. Any ideas?"

I remembered something. "Grandpa was planning a vacation to New Mexico, someplace where he said something important had happened. Something to do with alien spaceships and nuclear testing."

"Where?"

"I don't know."

The gray line became a scar in the sky.

"Try to remember, Ronnie. We'll only have a few minutes once we're in EarthTwo's atmosphere."

The gray line was coming up fast. Could that be the rip in space that would lead back to my planet?

"Let's take a chance and go for it," said Tom.

He was definitely in my head. "If we make it, Tom, I'm going to make you sorry for doing that again."

"Let's hope you get the chance, Ronnie."

I yanked on the steering controls, flipping *Friendship One* on its side. I drove it straight toward the narrow gray rip in the sky.

FORTY-EIGHT

TOM
EN ROUTE TO ROSWELL, N.M.
1958

DIDN'T want to tell Ronnie what really worried me: How would we land? The pilot and the crew had taken off with the landing capsule, which usually splashes down in an ocean somewhere and gets picked up by NASA divers. Then the rocket ship crashes somewhere else in the ocean and gets fished out. But that wouldn't happen in 1958 when they barely even had a space program.

But maybe we were flying on a new kind of state-of-the-art rocket that could eject its landing capsule and still land itself. Otherwise, I could picture us smashing nose first into the ground and exploding. Whatever was left would become a secret, just a UFO to the government. And we would be toast. Really toast. *That's funny, Tom. Glad you still have your nasty sense of humor.*

Actually, that made me feel a little better.

I looked over at Ronnie, zoned in on steering the

ship, her hands clenched on the sticks, her blue eyes staring at the main forward screen, her lower lip caught between her teeth. She looked different now that I knew she was a girl. Was that just in my mind? She made more sense as a girl. Why hadn't I figured it out?

I had so many questions for Ronnie. I felt a little shy with her.

No time now.

The black rockets hadn't followed us. They were heading toward EarthOne, out of our rear-camera range.

There was a bump as we slipped through the gray rip. We entered EarthTwo's atmosphere. We didn't have much time. I was just going to have to hope the rocket could land and that Ronnie and I could figure out how to do it.

I imagined reeling back to the trip from EarthOne to Riverboat, when I'd been sitting in a seat behind the pilot, drilling into his mind for his knowledge about driving *Friendship One*. Then, I had imagined my mind a thumb drive plugged into the computer of his mind, copying everything from what I imagined was a pilot's manual. There had been humming and whizzing digits. Now I opened that thumb drive in my mind. There were instructions on *how* to land but nothing about *where* to land.

We couldn't go back to Nearmont, New Jersey, and

land behind the middle school in this baby. And no oceans, please, and no jungles.

Think. Hard. Rewind your mind.

I suddenly remembered something I had blurted out in Mrs. Rupp's history class. *"May 12, 1958. A thermonuclear explosion in New Mexico."*

"Ronnie, just what did Grandpa say happened in that place in New Mexico?"

"He wouldn't tell us anything except there'd been some rumors. I think he was afraid we'd say something in school. But he made Eddie memorize the name of the town and the coordinate numbers."

"Hold us steady."

I tried to tune Eddie in. He hadn't responded before, and I wasn't even sure he was okay. I held my breath and put all my energy into reaching through the universe for my brother. He tuned in pretty fast. *Phew.*

That you, bro? Where are you?

Looking for a landing site on EarthTwo. I'm so glad you're okay. But I'm in a hurry—you remember where Grandpa wanted to go on vacation in New Mexico?

It had a Spanish name.

Some clue.

It was on a map.

Did you see the map, Eddie?

Yeah.

So tell me where.

I don't have the map with me.

You don't need it. We have powers, Eddie. Rewind your mind back to the day you saw that map.

You kidding, Tom?

Just do it. We're going to crash.

Man, this is hard . . . got to focus . . . like a dream . . . my head hurts . . .

You can do it, Cap'n Eddie.

I could hear sounds—groaning maybe, and my head hurt as well. Twin-sense. It went on for a while. Then Eddie yelped.

Tom! I see Culebra de Cascabel. It's in a valley in the desert. The coordinate numbers are 106:06W and 34:19N.

Way to go! See you later, alligator.

"Ronnie," I said, "I just put some numbers on the GPS grid. Take us down."

FORTY-NINE

EVERYBODY on this planet was thin. Or at least they weren't fat. As soon as I realized this, I felt self-conscious. I thought, *I got to get me one of those loose shirts they wear, but in a superbig size so you can't tell what's underneath.* And then I suddenly stopped feeling self-conscious because I had this rageous thought: *If I am the only fat person on this planet, then I am not fat—I am special. Out of the ordinary, which is extraordinary.*

Think of it this way, Lessi: Back on EarthOne, EarthTwo, all the Earths if there are even more, there are tons (no pun intended) of fat people. Some are fatter than me, some aren't as fat, but we are all still fat. We are all in the fat group.

But here on Homeplace, I'm in a group called Alessa.

Oh, Lessi, there must be some weird air in this place to make you think stuff like this.

I woke up.

I was in a see-through cage. Four walls of glass. Thin

people in white coats walked past. There was a row of glass cages. The director, the Lump, the four soldiers, Britzky, and Buddy: each of them was in a separate glass cage. We were all wearing white gowns, like tents. Even Buddy. You couldn't tell anybody's size.

Britzky waved. We were too far away to talk.

"How are you doing, Alessa?" It was Dr. Traum in front of my cage. "We're just waiting for some tests to come back. Make sure you're not carrying anything that can infect the Primary People."

"What if we are?"

"We have medicine that can knock out most Earth viruses and bacteria," he said.

"Really? Like, I mean, the superhorrible diseases—the flu and smallpox, even AIDS?"

"Yes." He looked right at me because I guess he knew what I was going to say next.

"So how come you haven't wiped out those diseases on the Earths?"

"That's what Tom and Eddie's father asks the Council all the time." He started to walk away.

"Wait a minute, Dr. Traum. John Canty told us how you guys messed up your own planet, so why don't you want to help us? Some of it is your fault anyway."

He turned and came back. "You're a smart, bold girl, Alessa. I was impressed the way you pulled that Tech

Off! Day tour together. But this is way over your head. Sometimes the Primary People move in mysterious ways."

"What's mysterious about wanting to destroy us instead of help us?" I felt angry. It felt good. Better than feeling like a helpless prisoner in a glass cage.

"We have the entire universe to think of, not just two little planets."

"Two little planets that you didn't take care of like you were supposed to."

Dr. Traum sighed. "That is one way to look at it." His smile was sad. "We were not able to save ourselves. I am not sure we can save anyone else. Our bodies disintegrated along with our planet. We managed to preserve our rational minds, and we learned to take shapes, as you see, aided by machines. But we lost our powers to imagine and to empathize. We lost our humanity. That is why Tom and Eddie and their friends are so important to us."

"Important? The way you treat us?"

"We have been testing you, preparing you."

"For what?"

"For what happens next." He touched a switch on the wall, and the glass cages opened.

"What happens next?" I said.

"You and Todd will be slipping to EarthTwo. Tom and Ronnie are on their way. Eddie will be heading there soon. You will all meet in a terrible place called Culebra de Cascabel."

"Why?"

"A terrible thing happened there on EarthOne and must not happen on EarthTwo."

"What happened?"

"The Primary People had a chance to alter the course of the universe and we did not. We could not. We still cannot. But you give a second chance."

Just before he turned to walk away, I thought I saw tears in his green eyes.

FIFTY

CONCENTRATED on the landing instructions in the manual that the pilot had memorized and that I had scanned out of his head. Landing was one of the few things that *Friendship One* did not do automatically. There were buttons to push and levers to pull and commands to relay to Ronnie.

I was yelling, "Lift the nose," when we crashed.

Friendship One hit the desert sand and bounced up and settled back down with the sound of metal screaming like a humongous cat.

Then the plane shuddered. And was still.

I looked at Ronnie. She gave me a thumbs-up. I gave one back. If we'd been closer, we would have high-fived or bumped fists.

"Good job," she said. "For a boy."

Then we started giggling.

After a while, I said, "We should get out of here before people come."

"We need to find food and flashlights and stuff," she said, unbuckling her safety harness.

She was all business. I could see how she'd survived on her own, pretending to be a boy, living on the street. I didn't mind following her around even if she was a girl.

We found a supply closet with backpacks marked NASA. Inside were medical kits, water bottles, ready-to-eat food, flashlights, flares, a tent, and blankets. I found a pistol in the closet, but Ronnie and I looked at each other and shook our heads. We didn't know how to use it, and we weren't going to shoot anybody anyway. We opened a hatch. A plastic slide dropped out and we slid down into the desert.

It was late afternoon. The sun was going down and I could already feel chilliness in the air.

It was beautiful in an eerie kind of way. White clouds shaped like mythological animals hung in the darkening blue sky, and I thought I heard a distant singing, which was probably the wind. There were mountains in the distance. They seemed to be moving, coming closer. Mirages.

"It's beautiful," said Ronnie. "Weird."

"We should get away from the plane. People may have seen it come down."

"Which way?"

I pointed to the sun dropping behind the mountains to my left. "That's west, so"—I turned halfway to the right— "that must be north. That's where Culebra de Cascabel is."

"How do you know?"

"It was in Eddie's mind."

"Do you know everything that's in his mind?"

In what was left of the light, I could see that Ronnie's face was scrunched up, as if she was worried about something. "I don't know for sure. Why?"

"Well, if it goes both ways, then he knows what's in your mind."

I understood what she was getting at, and I was glad. Maybe I'm more sensitive than people give me credit for. "You're worried about whether he knows you're a girl."

"I'd like to tell him myself."

"I'll try not to think about it. Let's go north."

"One more thing," she said. "I guess you didn't take Spanish in school."

"French. Why?"

"*Culebra de Cascabel* means 'rattlesnake.'"

"You think I'm afraid of snakes?"

We hoisted the backpacks and walked north until it got dark. I'd read about how night falls on the desert like a lid slamming down on a pot, but I'd always thought it was just a writer being fancy. And then *bang!* One minute there was light in the sky; the next minute it was totally black. I dug out a flashlight, mostly to scare away snakes.

Ronnie and I didn't talk. We were both too tired. We were stumbling along, almost too tired to stop, if that makes any sense. We almost walked into a mountain. Or maybe it was just a little hill. Suddenly, there was a wall of rock and dirt in front of us.

"Here," I said. It was all I could say.

We spread two blankets on the ground and wrapped them around us. It was cold. We were too tired to make a fire. We drank water. Ronnie took out one of the ready-to-eat packages. "It's meatloaf," she said.

"Anything else?"

"An energy bar." She broke it in half and handed me a piece.

We ate the bar and fell asleep shivering.

In my dream, I wasn't cold.

There was a fire, bright and hot, and when I sat up, I saw shapes around the fire. They looked like the Council members we had seen on the grandstand in Riverboat.

"Why am I here?" I asked.

"To stop the atomic explosion. Tomorrow, May 12, 1958,

there will be an atomic explosion that will convince the U.S. government to continue testing nuclear bombs. It must be stopped."

"Why can't you stop it?"

"The Primary People will never intervene in the affairs of an Earth."

"I'm a Primary Person."

"You're a halfie. You can do anything you want."

I woke up. It was morning. Ronnie was already up, staring at the last burning embers of a fire.

"Did you start this?" she asked.

"No, but I had the weirdest dream," I said.

"What's that?" she asked, pointing.

Neatly folded on the ground were two long white shirts.

"It wasn't a dream," I said softly. "The Council came down to tell me I had to stop the atomic explosion today."

"How?"

"I don't know."

Ronnie grinned at me. "You'll figure it out, Tom. You always do."

We scattered the embers of the fire, rolled our blankets, and put on the long white shirts. I could feel the heat reflecting off the desert as the sun rose.

The hill we had camped against turned out to be one

in a line of hills that rose into a mountain. We headed north through a canyon and into another part of the desert that looked like a huge lake of sand.

There were giant signs on poles dug into the sand.

NO ADMITTANCE

CULEBRA DE CASCABEL

ATOMIC TESTING GROUNDS

FIFTY-ONE

EDDIE
WASHINGTON, D.C.
2012

THE covered wagon was parked near the Washington Monument, and Grandpa was sitting on the front seat. He winked and nodded at the seat next to him.

Get on. Be cool.

I swallowed down all the questions I had for him. *What happened? Where'd he been? Where'd I been?*

I had a headache. I remembered jumping on the back of Hercules's bike, but that seemed like days ago. I remembered Dad and Riverboat and speaking to the Council and the trip to Homeplace and how much my head had hurt from trying to remember those names and numbers in New Mexico for Tom.

New Mexico. Tom and Ronnie were there. On EarthTwo in 1958. How did I know that?

I climbed up onto the front seat. One of the Browns

started the SUV and the wagon began to move. A Brown was walking along on each side of the wagon. They talked into their sleeves. "We are moving."

I felt peculiar, as if I was there and not there.

Grandpa nudged me. *You're here and you're not here. Get used to it.*

Erin hurried up alongside the wagon. "We were so worried about you, Tom. What was going through your mind?"

"About what?"

"Jumping on that motorcycle," she said. "Thank goodness you had that helmet on."

"Who was that biker guy?" asked a Brown.

"What biker guy?" I said. He must mean Hercules.

"He doesn't remember anything," said Erin. "It's common after a coma."

"A coma?" I said.

"You were in a coma for twenty-four hours," said Erin. "In the hospital for three days."

I floated a thought to Grandpa. *What's up?*

Primary People can be two places at the same time, Eddie, remember?

Homeplace and the hospital?

Right.

Like when you were in the nursing home on EarthOne with Tommy and living with me on EarthTwo?

That's it, Eddie.

How can that be?

One is really you and one is your projection, your hologram.

How can I tell the difference, Grandpa?

Takes concentration and practice, Eddie.

What am I now?

Figure it out.

I pinched myself. It hurt. I was me.

"So who was the biker?" the same Brown asked again.

I shrugged at him but slipped a thought into his mind. *That was Injun Joe. I was following him. He murdered Dr. Robinson.*

"What?" The Brown turned to the other Brown, who gave him a funny look.

Now, this is super groovy, I thought. *I can keep them off balance.* I wondered if I could mess with the minds of linebackers blitzing me. *C'mon, Eddie, no football right now.*

"We were so scared when you fell off," said Erin.

"I fell off?"

"We told the media you were exhausted," said Erin.

I nudged Grandpa. *Am I somewhere else now, too?*

Your hologram is heading to Culebra de Cascabel.

I'm going too.

The Browns were muttering about the murder of a doctor named Robinson all the way back to the White House. *Let's hear it for Mark Twain!*

FIFTY-TWO

T HE slip from Homeplace to EarthTwo was a lousy ride, two hours that felt like two days of chills and nausea before we were dumped out onto the desert. The flu symptoms disappeared the moment we landed, but then the heat dropped over us like plastic bags.

Alessa and I were standing on a hill overlooking a canyon that cut through a mountain and ended in an ocean of sand. There were huge signs in the desert.

NO ADMITTANCE

CULEBRA DE CASCABEL

ATOMIC TESTING GROUNDS

"We better get out of here," said Alessa.

"Too late."

I pointed down. A caravan of army trucks and jeeps, even a tank, rumbled over the sandy road through the canyon, sending up clouds of dust. Soldiers with guns walked alongside.

A helicopter was clattering up ahead. It made so much noise and churned up so much sand that we didn't see Eddie suddenly appear next to us. Buddy was at his feet.

"Wassup, dudes?"

"Eddie," screamed Alessa, throwing her arms around him. All she got was air.

"Hologram," I said. "Where's the real Eddie?"

"He'll be here," said Eddie. "Look!"

Below us, the army caravan had come out of the canyon onto the desert floor and stopped.

Ronnie and Tom were blocking the way.

"What are they doing?" asked Alessa.

"Trying to stop the testing," said Eddie.

"They can't," said Alessa. "It already happened."

"Not on this planet," I said.

"Even if they stop it for today," she said, "what about the future?"

"Who knows? You ever hear of the butterfly effect?" I said.

"Some little thing causes bigger things to happen

and changes history," said Eddie. "Like if they don't test today, maybe they'll have a meeting and decide atomic bombs are a bad thing."

"How'd you know that?" I said.

"You think you're the only person who knows anything?" said Alessa.

I didn't want to say it out loud, but I thought, *Well, most of the time . . .*

"Hey," shouted Alessa.

Eddie and Buddy were racing down the mountain toward the caravan.

We ran after them.

FIFTY-THREE

TOM
CULEBRA DE CASCABEL, N.M.
1958

AGUY with a gold braid on his Smokey Bear hat got out of a jeep and started walking toward us.

"I'm Colonel Kirby Yorke of the United States Army," he yelled. "You kids can't be here."

A voice that sounded like Dr. Traum said to me, *Speak for the Primary People, Thomas.*

I was scared. I wished I had my Extreme-Temperature Narrow-Beam Climate Simulators. All I had was my mind.

You can do it, Tommy. That was Dad.

"Move out, kids." The colonel swung his arm. Everything—his men and the tank and the jeeps and trucks—arranged themselves in a row facing us.

Ronnie nudged me. "There's Eddie! And Buddy."

They were skidding down the mountain as if they were sand surfing. I was so happy to see my brother. I was even happy to see that dog. But I had to work fast.

I imagined a powerful voice. It came out of my mouth like a bullhorn. "That's far enough, Colonel. There will be no atomic testing today."

"Who are you?" he yelled.

The row of army vehicles started coming toward us. A helicopter circled above us.

I imagined the helicopter descending, then tilting so that its whirling blades churned the air a few feet off the desert floor. Giant plumes of sand rose like geysers in front of me and Ronnie.

"Groovy," said Eddie, appearing beside me. "Dig this."

The sand geysers began to sway like hula dancers.

"Cool," I said. I was trying to imagine what I could do to top the hula dancers when I saw Alessa and Britzky running toward us. "Ronnie! Get them out of the way, behind the rocks. You too."

She hesitated until Eddie said, "Yeah, we've got a plan."

What plan, Eddie?

I figured you had one.

We waited until Ronnie, Alessa, and Britzky were out of sight before we let the sandstorm subside.

Now it was just the two of us facing the colonel and his advancing army. And I could tell it was only Eddie's hologram.

"That's far enough, Colonel," I roared.

The line kept moving closer. We could see the faces of the soldiers.

"Yo, Smokey," Eddie roared. "You heard my homey."

Do you have to talk like that? said Dr. Traum. *This is about the fate of the world.*

We're doing it our way, Eddie and I said together. We high-fived. *It's twin time.*

"I said, who the hell are you?" boomed the colonel.

"We represent the people of the Earths who don't want the Doomsday Clock to hit midnight," we said.

"You're just two little boys interfering with the federal government of these United States of America."

Just two little boys? Eddie and I looked at each other and got the same idea at the same time. Twin-sense! *How about more little boys?*

When we finished laughing, there were four of us.

One of the Eddies said, *Can we make more?*

My hologram said, **You're not as dumb as you look.**

I said, **I think we can make as many holograms as we want.**

Let's find out.

My head really hurt, but then there were eight of us. And four Buddys!

"We are from the Primary People," I boomed, "and we have come to stop the atomic testing. It will only lead to more war and suffering and the destruction of the planet."

"You are all under arrest."

All sixteen of us? And eight Buddys?

Count me in, said the real Eddie, popping up beside me.

We're all real, said one of my holograms.

Whatever, said the real Eddie.

There were thirty-two of us and sixteen Buddys.

"Now, you listen to me, you misguided do-gooders," yelled the colonel. "I don't care what kind of tricks you think you're playing, but you have thirty seconds to clear this area before we take you by force." He signaled the tank to aim its gun at us.

At all sixty-four of us? And thirty-two Buddys?

"Detail," roared the colonel. "Forward, ho-oh."

Sounds like John Wayne.

Does that make us the Indians?

Whatever.

FIFTY-FOUR

RONNIE

CULEBRA DE CASCABEL, N.M.

1958

WHAT's going on?" said Alessa.

"I don't know," said Britzky.

That was a first.

I didn't know either.

The row of trucks and jeeps, with the tank in the middle and the soldiers behind, moved over the desert toward Tom, Eddie, and Buddy and their three holograms. The six of them looked so small.

The colonel, the guy in the Smokey Bear hat, was marching by himself up front. He looked as if he thought he was the hero in a movie.

The whole thing looked like a movie.

Except I was scared.

"This is your final warning," yelled the colonel. "Leave the area immediately. All of you." He ran his pointing finger across the horizon.

Britzky said, "Could he be seeing more of them than we do?"

"Like imaginary Toms and Eddies and Buddys?" said Alessa. "In their minds?"

"We're staying right here until you call off the test," yelled Eddie.

Somehow I could tell he was the real Eddie, not a hologram Eddie. I felt so proud of him. And then I remembered that he didn't know the truth about me.

One of the two Toms waved his arms, and the gun on the tank rose up and pointed at the helicopter. It flew away.

The soldiers began whirling around suddenly, as if they were being surrounded by hundreds of Toms, Eddies, and Buddys in a giant circle.

"I wish we could see this," said Britzky.

"Then the twins would be controlling your mind too," I said.

"Be worth it."

The soldiers dropped their guns and began to dance in the circle we couldn't see.

"Let's go," shouted Alessa. Britzky and I followed her out from behind the rocks. The real Tom and Eddie ran out to meet us. They grabbed our arms and pulled us into the circle.

"How many are there?" I asked Tom.

"A couple hundred," said Tom. "I lost count."

"Why can't we see them?"

"They're in the soldiers' heads."

I didn't know how long we danced and sang, but the heat was leaving the desert and night was beginning to fall when we fell too, exhausted.

The colonel never joined us. He just plopped down onto the sand and cried.

Suddenly, the soldiers began screaming and racing back to their trucks and jeeps as if they were being chased by . . . rattlesnakes!

Because they were!

Dozens of snakes burst out of the sand and began slithering forward, rattling.

"That is so brilliant," said Britzky. "What powers!"

"They're real," screamed Tom and Eddie. They were paralyzed.

I remembered the flares in the backpacks we had carried from the plane. I made a circle of flares around us and lit them. The snakes stayed outside the circle of fire.

I was standing in the light of one of the flares, feeling proud of myself, when Eddie took a hard look at me and said, "Why are you dressed like a girl?"

• • •

Very impressive.

It seems like the Earths have earned another chance, Dr. Traum.

What do you have in mind, John?

Hold up on the decision for a year. See what else they can do.

Let me talk to the Council. I have a feeling they can be persuaded.

FIFTY-FIVE

W E were sitting in the sand around a fire, sharing the food we had taken from the plane, when Grandpa suddenly appeared like a mirage in the desert. I couldn't tell if it was him or his hologram.

"Good news," he said. "The testing was called off. The Council was very impressed. You bought the Earths another year of survival."

"Yesss!" said Britzky, jumping up. He grabbed Alessa and Ronnie. The three of them hopped up and down.

"Not so fast," said Grandpa. "You're going to have to do much more in the next year to convince them further, and you're going to have to do it here on this planet. We can't take the chance right now of sending anybody back to 2012. Those two agents, Mathison and Quinn, are in Washington. With the Lump and the director. They know Tom and Eddie are twin halfies."

Britzky and Alessa looked at each other and dropped their heads. I could feel their gloom.

"Don't feel bad," I said. "It would have come out. You guys are great."

That was nice. For Tom.

I traced the thought to Ronnie. If she felt a tickle in her mind, she didn't scowl at me.

"Will we ever get back home?" said Alessa.

"Hard to say," said Grandpa. "Might depend on what you do here."

"Just think," I said, "you won't have to give that report on the tour to the middle-school assembly."

Nobody cracked a smile at that. I could sense dark clouds in the minds of Britzky and Alessa. They were feeling sad about their families, wondering when they would see them again. I thought about my stepmom. I had barely thought about her in the past week, so much had happened. I knew she cared about me. I would find a way to get a message to her, to Alessa's and Britzky's families, too. *Don't worry. We're all right. Just busy saving the world.*

Grandpa stood up. "We better get going. There's a small vehicle in *Friendship One* we can use to get out of this area after we blow up the spacecraft. Can't let the 1958 space-agency guys find a 2012 rocket ship."

I looked over at Eddie. He hadn't eaten much—he was just holding on to Buddy and staring down.

You okay?

How could he lie to me for so long?

It's she.

Whatever. Eddie was having a hard time with Ronnie as a girl. He had barely talked to her or looked at her.

"He's old-fashioned," said Alessa to me, noticing Eddie's unhappiness. "It's going to take him a while."

"It's no big deal," said Britzky. "I always thought Ronnie was a girl."

Ronnie smiled. "If you're so smart," she said, "what are we going to do now?"

"Lots to do on this planet," said Britzky. "Check the timeline. We could be freedom riders."

"Freedom riders?" repeated Ronnie.

"They rode buses in the South to fight against racial segregation," said Alessa.

"Count me in," said Ronnie.

"It's dangerous," said Grandpa. "People get killed fighting for what's right."

I said, "Mark Twain said, 'The trouble is not in dying for a friend, but in finding a friend worth dying for.'"

I liked the way everybody looked at me and gave me

a fist or a thumbs-up. Except for Eddie. He just sat there, cross-legged in the sand. I couldn't get into his mind. Lockdown.

I went over and gave him a light punch on the shoulder. Buddy growled at me. Trying to get Eddie to smile, I yelled, "Raiders rule!"

Eddie sighed but he didn't look up. I wasn't sure why he felt so hurt. I guess I'm still not a touchy-feely guy.

The team needs you, Cap'n Eddie. When his head came up slowly, I said, *Don't let us down.*

He looked at Ronnie. "Why didn't you trust me?"

"I didn't trust anybody," said Ronnie.

"Veronica had her reasons," said Alessa, giving Ronnie a squeeze. They looked like old friends. Old girlfriends. "I'm sure she'll tell you someday."

Ronnie walked over to Eddie and put her hand out. "I'm sorry, Eddie. I was afraid you would hate me."

He took her hand and stood up. "How could I hate you? My sidekick. My best friend."

"Group hug," yelled Alessa.

I thought Buddy licked my leg but I wasn't sure.

"Freedom riders," said Eddie. He was still holding Ronnie's hand. He winked at her. "We'll probably need a freedom driver."

"Yo, bro, way to go," I shouted.

I realized I was starting to talk like Eddie. He was laughing when he thought back at me, *You have to talk like that?*